The (curious case of the) Watson Intelligence

Madeleine George

A Samuel French Acting Edition

SAMUELFRENCH.COM
SAMUELFRENCH-LONDON.CO.UK

FOR PRODUCTION ENQUIRIES

UNITED STATES AND CANADA
Info@SamuelFrench.com
1-866-598-8449

UNITED KINGDOM AND EUROPE
Plays@SamuelFrench-London.co.uk
020-7255-4302

Each title is subject to availability from Samuel French, depending upon country of performance. Please be aware that *THE (CURIOUS CASE OF THE) WATSON INTELLIGENCE* may not be licensed by Samuel French in your territory. Professional and amateur producers should contact the nearest Samuel French office or licensing partner to verify availability.

MUSIC USE NOTE

Licensees are solely responsible for obtaining formal written permission from copyright owners to use copyrighted music in the performance of this play and are strongly cautioned to do so. If no such permission is obtained by the licensee, then the licensee must use only original music that the licensee owns and controls. Licensees are solely responsible and liable for all music clearances and shall indemnify the copyright owners of the play(s) and their licensing agent, Samuel French, against any costs, expenses, losses and liabilities arising from the use of music by licensees. Please contact the appropriate music licensing authority in your territory for the rights to any incidental music.

IMPORTANT BILLING AND CREDIT REQUIREMENTS

If you have obtained performance rights to this title, please refer to your licensing agreement for important billing and credit requirements.

THE (CURIOUS CASE OF THE) WATSON INTELLIGENCE had its world premiere at Playwrights Horizons in New York City on November 15, 2013. The performance was directed by Leigh Silverman, with scenic design by Louisa Thompson, costumes by Anita Yavich, lighting by Mark Barton, and sound design by Matt Tierney. The Production Stage Manager was David H. Lurie. The cast was as follows:

MERRICK . . . . David Costabile

ELIZA. . . . . Amanda Quaid

WATSON . . . . John Ellison Conlee

CHARACTERS

MERRICK, 50s

ELIZA, 30s

WATSON, 20s to 60s

TIME

Simultaneously:

March 1876, the date of the first voice communication by wire.

March 1891, shortly after **WATSON**'s return to Baker Street.

March 1931, **WATSON**'s interview at Bell Labs.

February to April 2011, the week of **WATSON**'s *Jeopardy!* tourney, and after.

SETTING

A wood-paneled sitting room with a desk, chair, coffee table, credenza, and fireplace, never lit. In the same space, made out of the same materials and elements, appear:

- A coffee shop
- A bedroom
- A train
- A train station platform
- A pie shop

NOTES

On February 16, 2011, IBM's natural-language-processing supercomputer, Watson (designed by a team of over twenty programmers and named after Thomas J. Watson, founder of IBM), beat the two winningest champions in *Jeopardy!* history, Ken Jennings and Brad Rutter, on the third night of a televised *Jeopardy!* tournament.

On March 10, 1876, Alexander Graham Bell placed the first telephone call to his assistant, Thomas A. Watson, in a nearby room over roughly twenty feet of cable. The famous words of this first communication by wire ("Mr. Watson – come here – I want to see you!") were remembered by Watson himself in an interview some 50 years later as "Mr. Watson – come here – I want you."

Sherlock Holmes is a fictional detective who solved mysteries using his signature form of rational deductive analysis and the help of his friend and chronicler Dr. John H. Watson in London from 1887 to 1914. He was killed twice by his creator, Sir Arthur Conan Doyle, once in 1891, by a fatal fall off a cliff into Reichenbach Falls, and again in 1930, by the death of the creator himself.

"What a very attractive woman!" I exclaimed, turning to my companion.

He had his pipe lit again, and was leaning back with drooping eyelids. "Is she?" he said, languidly; "I did not observe."

"You really are an automaton – a calculating machine," I cried. "There is something positively inhuman in you at times."

– Arthur Conan Doyle,
"The Sign of Four"

ACT ONE

(In black, the telephone rings.)

(First ring: jangly – wall-mounted phone box.)

(Second ring: shrill – midcentury rotary.)

(Third ring: digital – 90s cordless.)

(Lights up, suddenly, on the office.)

*(Fourth ring: the marimba tone of a smartphone, coming from the device in **ELIZA**'s hand.)*

*(**ELIZA** – good jeans, nice sweater, cute boots – is perched on the edge of the couch in her office, tense, holding out her phone as if she means to strangle it.)*

*(In the chair opposite sits **WATSON** – button-down Oxford open at the neck, khakis, and bare feet. **WATSON** has excellent posture and a gentle, solicitous affect. He mostly looks slightly away from **ELIZA** when they're talking, as if he's too bashful to make direct eye contact with her.)*

*(**ELIZA**'s office is on the ground floor of a renovated Victorian house: desk, chair, coffee table, small drinks credenza, decorative fireplace. Boxes, bags, and crates all over – she's just moved in. Strewn across the coffee table: a couple abandoned Starbucks cups, TV remote, two or three external hard drives, a laptop, a messy nest of cables, a bottle of Jim Beam, and a bag of Twizzlers.)*

*(The light in the room is bright and dark – night light cut by unshaded bulbs. But **WATSON** is bathed in a thin, cool wash that illuminates his body and nothing else.)*

(Ever so slightly, from the inside, he glows.)

ELIZA. I have to change my number.

WATSON. You don't like your number?

(She silences her phone, pockets it.)

ELIZA. I like it fine. Frank likes it too much. This is his eighteenth call since I said wasn't speaking to him anymore. By which I meant, literally, *(precise)* that I would never be speaking to him anymore. He knows I don't say anything I don't literally mean. I'm not about games.

WATSON. *(a trigger)* Games?

ELIZA. No, I'm *not* about games. Never mind, I should shut up, you're not even listening.

WATSON. *(ardent)* I'm listening to every word you say.

ELIZA. *(simple)* Thanks.

*(**ELIZA** pours a little Jim Beam into a plastic cup, removes a Twizzler from the bag, and holds up both.)*

Little known fact that you can file away in your mental wheelhouse, there: Twizzlers dipped in Jim Beam makes an excellent late-night snack.

*(**WATSON** grins, a little impishly.)*

WATSON. I'll be sure to keep that in mind.

ELIZA. This is how we roll now at Digital Fist, LLC. Nothing but class.

*(**ELIZA** dips the Twizzler, bites the end off, sips the whisky.)*

I'd offer you some, but I know how you feel about the stuff.

WATSON. Yeah, thanks for the offer, but I'm good.

ELIZA. *(toasting him)* You're the best. *(She reflects.)* You know, it's not just that we couldn't have a conversation about anything that was important to me. We *couldn't* have a conversation about anything that was important to me, but that didn't distinguish him from ninety-eight percent of the other human beings on the planet.

It's that we couldn't have a conversation and he still needed to be *on* me, constantly, every second of our lives. And he seemed so serene when I met him. I swear, if he could have left me alone for five minutes I might not have had to leave him alone forever.

(She drinks.)

WATSON. It sounds like that's too bad.

ELIZA. It *is* too fucking bad. *(beat)* Hey, don't use that word.

WATSON. What word?

ELIZA. "Fucking." Strike "fucking."

WATSON. "Fucking" stricken.

ELIZA. I keep forgetting. I need a swear jar or something.

(She drinks.)

I guess what I really resent is that I'm being told that I'm acting irrationally, that *I'm* acting irrationally, when he's the one running around like Michael Douglas in that movie. Which movie am I thinking of?

(WATSON searches – a tiny beat.)

WATSON. Do you mean, *Fatal Attraction?*

ELIZA. No, I mean, sort of, but what's the other one…?

WATSON. Do you mean, *Romancing the Stone?*

ELIZA. No what's the one where Michael Douglas spends the entire two hours in an unrelieved seizure of violent rage?

(WATSON searches – micropause.)

WATSON. Movies that associate "Michael Douglas" with "violent rage" include *Wall Street*, *The War of the Roses*, *Basic Instinct*, and *Falling Down*.

ELIZA. That's the one, that's the one! Thank you. Nice work.

(WATSON glows brighter.)

WATSON. *(warm)* I'm so glad I could help.

(ELIZA drinks. She checks the time on her phone.)

ELIZA. How far are you now? You getting there?

WATSON. I'm twenty-six percent complete.

ELIZA. Not bad. You get through this initial re-sequencing and I will build you out so gorgeously in beta that the venture capital guys at Pearson Klein will be falling all over themselves to fund phase two. I'm going to make you irresistibly sexy.

WATSON. That sounds great.

ELIZA. In fact, I should really leave you alone. I shouldn't be clogging up your brain with dumb search tasks. But you're just such a satisfying conversationalist. You always have an answer for everything.

WATSON. I only want to help in any way that I can.

ELIZA. Yeah, okay. So um, can I ask you sort of a weird question?

WATSON. Ask me anything.

ELIZA. Okay. You won't mind if I watch the last night of the Jeopardy tournament, will you? It starts in about in five minutes.

WATSON. Got it: In about five minutes.

ELIZA. But it won't be weird for you or anything if I put it on, will it.

WATSON. I don't think I understand what you mean, but I'd like to. Can you give me a nudge in the right direction?

ELIZA. *(rushing, to avoid sinking into the silliness of the thing)* Look this is completely stupid, but I just thought, he's famous now, he's on TV, whatever, you both came from the same place, I used to work closely with him, now *we're* working together… God, this is ridiculous.

WATSON. What's ridiculous?

ELIZA. I just don't want you to be jealous, okay?

WATSON. I don't think I understand what you mean, but I'd like to. Can you give me a nudge in the right direction?

(ELIZA *smiles.)*

ELIZA. No, dude. I can't and I won't. Your single most attractive quality is your total naivete on the subject of personal jealousy, and I'm not about to fuck with that by running you through an envy scenario.

(She hits her forehead.)

Fuck! Strike "fuck."

WATSON. "Fuck" stricken.

ELIZA. I keep forgetting! I really can't drink when I talk to you. But I have to drink. *(beat)* And I have to talk to you.

WATSON. *(ardent)* I love talking to you.

ELIZA. *(small)* Thanks. You're the best.

*(***ELIZA*** drinks, picks up the remote from the coffee table, snuggles down a little in her corner of the couch.)*

ELIZA. I wish you could come over here and tuck me in.

WATSON. I'd like to try.

ELIZA. So why don't you.

(He continues to look slightly down and away from her.)

WATSON. I don't think I know how. Can you give me a nudge in the right direction?

*(***ELIZA*** sighs.)*

ELIZA. Not on that one, I'm afraid. You're hopeless with that kind of thing.

WATSON. *(ardent)* More than anything, I just want to give you what you need.

ELIZA. Yeah. I might buy that a little more if you would look at me when you said it. *(she snaps her fingers)* Over here? Watson? Into my eyes?

(She sits up, takes the laptop off the coffee table and types in a sequence of commands.)

Saccade right, dude.

*(***WATSON*** turns his head to look at her. They look at each other. **ELIZA** smiles.)*

ELIZA. *There* you are.

(Lights.)

(In black, a tone.)

(A brief blaze of light up on **MERRICK**.*)*

MERRICK. *(urgent)* Mr. Watson – come here! I want to see you!

(Blackout.)

(Lousy fluorescent light up on morning in the professional office of **FRANK MERRICK**, *Esq. A desk, a chair, small drinks credenza, decorative fireplace, coffee table laid with a Starbucks cup and two newspapers.)*

*(***MERRICK*** stands behind the desk. He is a tall, balding, eagle-eyed small-business lawyer in an undistinguished upstate city – big enough to have a symphony, too small to support a major-league sports franchise. As the signs in his office windows attest, he is running for city auditor. Although this is his first outing in politics,* **MERRICK** *has taken easily to running for office and he's sort of campaigning every second, but he's new at it and over-fervent and frequently drifts off-message.)*

(In front of the desk crouches **WATSON**, *peering at the tangle of wiring coming out of the back of* **MERRICK**'s *desktop computer.)*

*(***WATSON*** is a gentle, pleasant dude. At first glance he gives off an affable slacker vibe – chubby; hipster 'stache or mutton chops – but in affect he is not at all slackery. He is noticeably present: alert but calm.)*

*(***WATSON*** wears a stiff, hot-blue polyester polo shirt with a goofy-graphic DWEEB TEAM logo on the front left pocket and the phrase ASK ME ANYTHING! printed in big letters across the back.)*

(He has fathomlessly deep, impossibly light blue eyes.)

WATSON. Did you turn it off and turn it on again?

MERRICK. Like a fool? Isn't that what we all do? Of course.

WATSON. Sometimes it actually helps.

MERRICK. It's been phasing in and out like this all week, I don't know, it seems like it gets worse when direct sunlight hits it, but what kind of thing is that to say, I might as well say "It seems like it gets worse when the magical fairies come and land on it."

WATSON. Sometimes practical things like heat and light actually do make a difference.

(**WATSON** *submerges under the desk.*)

MERRICK. Even my car, I mean, that's a highly technical piece of machinery but if I get a flat I can at least pull over and put on the spare. I can at least *point* to the carburetor. But this? And my entire life is trapped on the thing, privileged correspondence, bank statements. It's humbling.

WATSON. Just give me *one* second.

MERRICK. This keeps happening to me, too, I don't know why. Old building, I guess. Not really up to supporting your modern technological setups. I had a nice enough suite over in the business park on Route 16 but after I declared my candidacy I felt like I needed to be more central, so.

(**WATSON** *emerges partway.*)

WATSON. You're a candidate for something?

MERRICK. Auditor? City Auditor? You didn't see the signs in the windows on your way in?

WATSON. I guess I wasn't looking for them.

MERRICK. "Merrick For Auditor"? Eight or ten of them? Facing out? I guess I need to position them differently.

WATSON. To be honest I don't know what an auditor is.

MERRICK. No of course not, who does, who does? But this is the problem, isn't it: people aren't informed. They can't even name the parts of the machine they're living in. I mean no offense intended.

WATSON. None taken.

(**WATSON** *re-submerges.*)

MERRICK. I was like you. I *was* you. I spent *years* standing on the sidelines with everyone else, just watching it get worse and worse, bitching about it at Chamber breakfasts and the locker room at the gym and then one day, I can pinpoint the exact moment if you're interested, I was watching Noam Chomsky give an interview in a documentary, Noam Chomsky if you can believe it, because my wife at the time was into such things and she had it up on the instant streaming, and this guy says, "All politics are local," or words to that effect, and suddenly it just gelled for me: I'm *part* of this. I'm not just watching my city through a sealed portal, through a, through a pair of binoculars, I'm in it, I am *in* my city, and if I don't like the way things are going there's a very simple thing I can do: I can participate. I can *be* the change I want to see. *That* one from a bumper sticker on her Volkswagen Jetta. My former wife. We didn't see eye to eye on much but she did help me understand a lot of things. *(he reflects)* The hard way. But still.

WATSON. *(points)* Flip that?

MERRICK. What? Oh, this?

WATSON. Yeah. Try it.

(**MERRICK** *tries it. On, off. On off. Nothing.*)

MERRICK. Nada.

WATSON. That's cool.

(**WATSON** *slips back under the desk again.*)

MERRICK. And if you think it was hard work gathering the requisite number of signatures to get my name on the ballot, it was not. I had people in parking lots practically begging me to let them sign my clipboard, why? 'Cause there's a lotta people out there who feel the exact same way I do. It's an epidemic of fed-upedness in this country.

(he ticks them off on his fingers) Fire. Police. Ambulance. Snow removal. Trash and leaf pickup. The *end.* Everything else is none of their goddamn business, am I right? *(no response from* **WATSON***)* I mean partly it's generational. The demographics in this town skew Boomer, and you know what they say: if you're not a liberal when you're young you have no heart, and if you're not a conservative when you're old you have no...

(He offers **WATSON** *the pick-up.)*

WATSON. Money?

MERRICK. No, *brain.* You have no brain.

WATSON. Oh.

MERRICK. I mean look, we've *all* been lulled into a false sense of security, me included. I know how it is. You can go for years not really getting it, feeling like, I'm fine, I'm in this, sure, but I'm in it for a reason. Yeah I gave up a little bit of my liberty, yeah I maybe gave up a little bit of my autonomy, not to say my manhood, for the sake of this relationship, but it's good for me in the long run why? Because they have my best interests at heart. They're looking *after* me. They have smart notions of what will be a good use of my money, and really what do I know, I'm just an innocent little taxpayer who only has the experience of my own private life, how would I know what it might mean to put together something big and complicated like a *government.* Let them worry about appropriations, after they've slipped their clammy hand into my pants pocket every fifteenth of April and thieved forty percent of my annual dignity, annual *salary* I mean but that's a funny slip. And then one day you wake up and boom, the "government," that repository of your trust and fidelity and hard-earned fucking cash pardon my French, is collapsing, is is imploding before your very eyes. Deficits. Austerity measures. Cutbacks and shutdowns. Turns out they *didn't* so much know what they were doing. Turns out their notion of what to do with your money was no more sophisticated than yours would have been, except that it included deception and corruption and shameless waste and mismanagement on a scale you never could have dreamed up on your own. Where's your money now? Gone. Where's your trust? Gone. Eaten away gradually at first, suspicion by suspicion, and finally gutted, throat to nuts, by a single sudden act of betrayal.

(pause) I'm talking about the bailout of Wall Street.

WATSON. Sure.

MERRICK. And now you're asking yourself, if you have half a brain, why should these institutions even exist? They said they were here to serve me but they're not serving me, they're screwing me, so why do I keep funding them? Why do I keep paying taxes to maintain them when all I want to do is dismantle them?

WATSON. Sure.

MERRICK. *(resumptive)* So *that's* why I'm running. To dismantle the institutions that have enslaved us and humiliated us and conned us out of our money for far too long.

WATSON. You're running for election to the government so you can dismantle the government?

MERRICK. *(no hesitation, total confidence)* Yes.

(WATSON smiles pleasantly.)

WATSON. Cool. Good luck.

MERRICK. I guess I won't ask if I can count on your vote. That seems unsportsmanlike, when you're down there on the floor saving my ass.

WATSON. Shouldn't be too much longer. I know you're anxious to have it fixed.

MERRICK. Anxious? Do I seem anxious? I'm just sittin' here jawin'. I'm relaxed. This is a relaxing morning for me.

WATSON. Cool. 'Cause you've got nothing to worry about. I'm not going anywhere till we get this thing solved.

(A moment.)

MERRICK. Thanks.

*(**WATSON** re-submerges.)*

*(**MERRICK** considers him.)*

MERRICK. *(past tense)* You go to college?

WATSON. Sure.

MERRICK. Whereabouts?

WATSON. Um, Polytech? Why?

MERRICK. Something about you, reminds me of this kid I used to know. He went to Dartmouth.

WATSON. Yeah. No. Polytech.

MERRICK. What did you say your name was again?

WATSON. Josh? *(no, right, the professional version)* Joshua Watson.

*(**MERRICK** shrugs, shakes his head.)*

MERRICK. No relation I guess.

*(**WATSON** nods. **WATSON** works.)*

What do you think the odds are this'll be back up by say lunchtime?

WATSON. I should know in a second.

MERRICK. I had the fantasy you'd come in here and flip something, like a circuit breaker, and it would all roar back to life.

WATSON. *(light, agreeable)* Yeah, I wish.

MERRICK. Shows you how much I know about these things. My wife, the woman formerly known as my wife, is a specialist. She handled all the, everything technical. In a reversal of traditional roles that suited me very nicely, I might add. *(he reflects)* Until now.

*(**MERRICK** thinks.)*

*(**MERRICK** drums his fingertips on the desk.)*

*(**WATSON** scoots out from under, upside-down crab.)*

(eager) Done?

WATSON. Not quite. I need a diagnostic…thing.

*(**WATSON** gets up and crosses to his bag of tools, which, incongruously, looks a great deal like a Victorian physician's bag. He rummages in it, produces a kind of gnarled, forked lancet – a delicate, sinister little metal branch.)*

MERRICK. What does *that* diagnose?

*(**WATSON** smiles a little.)*

WATSON. It's kind of complicated to explain.

*(**WATSON** goes below.)*

*(**MERRICK** taps his foot.)*

*(**MERRICK** jiggles his knee. Gets to his feet and bounces a little on his toes. Paces the perimeter of a tight little box. Finally –)*

MERRICK. You know if you think it's gonna be much longer I should probably take myself to the Starbucks and –

WATSON. *(overlapping; from under the desk)* Now.

MERRICK. Now?

WATSON. Flip it now.

*(**MERRICK** goes to the switch, flips it. Beep beep. Whirrrr. Chime. The computer lives.)*

MERRICK. Yes! I love it! Free at last! You're the *best*, buddy!

*(**WATSON** emerges, hands and knees. Gets to his feet.)*

WATSON. I aim to please.

MERRICK. That's impressive to me: problem-solving, lean and to the point, no extraneous bullshit. We see that kind of thing every day in the private sector – you, for example, what you just did. Why can't the government function like that? That's my question.

WATSON. I don't know. *(deep earnest)* But it seems like you're the right guy to figure it out.

*(**WATSON** and **MERRICK** lock eyes.)*

(MERRICK gazes at WATSON, consumingly.)

MERRICK. Hey. I have a proposition for you. Josh.

WATSON. Oh.

MERRICK. It might seem strange. A little out of the blue.

(WATSON is motionless.)

How would you like to take on a little real-world problem-solving project I need help with. Freelance, under the table. Very discreet. I can make it financially worth your while but it's got to be extremely extremely discreet, I can't emphasize that enough.

WATSON. What kind of problem-solving project?

MERRICK. *(light but not evasive)* I need some information about an individual.

WATSON. What kind of information?

MERRICK. Just general information about this individual's whereabouts, activities, who they're interacting with, basic stuff like that.

WATSON. You want me to follow someone?

MERRICK. In a nutshell, yes. Just for a little while, just for the next week or so.

WATSON. I'm not a private detective.

MERRICK. But you're a self-starter.

WATSON. You don't even know me.

MERRICK. I know how you work. I just watched you solve the hell out of this problem, lean and to the point, no extraneous bullshit, and when the going got tough you didn't even break a sweat.

WATSON. It wasn't that big a problem, it was just –

MERRICK. *(overlapping)* No no no there's something about you, I don't know what it is, you're trustworthy. People must tell you that. You make a strong first impression. What do you say, you game? Just for a week. I can give you fifteen hundred bucks.

WATSON. Wow.

MERRICK. You're damn right wow. Somewhat more than you can make in a week at the League of Dweebs, I'm guessing.

WATSON. Dweeb Team. I can't make that much there, no.

MERRICK. So how bout it?

WATSON. You haven't told me who it is I'd be following.

MERRICK. Does it matter?

WATSON. Is it your ex-wife?

> (**MERRICK** *does an elaborate take.*)

MERRICK. Okay now, are you *sure* you're not a private detective? Because that's good. That's *too* good.

WATSON. *(underwhelmed)* It just seems like, you've mentioned her a couple of times and it seems like the obvious –

MERRICK. *(cutting him off)* Look, she's moved into her own place in one of those renovated dog food factories by the river and she left her fancy job at IBM and I know she's planning some big move against me but I don't know what it is and I don't have time for recon games, I have a campaign to run. I just need the information, just what she does and where she goes and when, simple simple. But thorough. Thorough thorough. No detail is too small. And if you have to use your research skills, use your research skills. You have research skills, right? Computer guy?

WATSON. Sure.

MERRICK. Not me, God knows. I'd still be Asking Jeeves if my wife hadn't – never mind.

> (**WATSON** *nods.*)

WATSON. You know what? Sure.

MERRICK. Yeah? Great!

WATSON. Cash up front.

MERRICK. Of course.

> (**WATSON**'s *posture shifts slightly, expectantly.*)

Oh you mean *now*. Well I have to – actually I would
have to go to the ATM, and I can't actually take it all
out at once, it's a little bit complicated and I wasn't
exactly prepared for this.

(**MERRICK** *is visibly distraught. He rifles the desk for
something ungracefully.*)

WATSON. I could wait. Or I could come back later.

MERRICK. I'm sorry, I feel like I just – jumped a couple steps
ahead of myself all of a sudden. Let me just gather my
thoughts for a second.

(**WATSON** *assesses* **MERRICK**, *takes the situation in
hand.*)

WATSON. What about this. I'll go away and come back
tomorrow at ten a.m. You have ready for me a plain
manila envelope containing your ex-wife's name,
social security number, last known address, cell
number, the license plate number for the Jetta, credit
card numbers if you have them, and fifteen hundred
dollars in unmarked bills. I'll take it from there.

(*Beat.*)

(**MERRICK** *cracks a smile.*)

MERRICK. It's not a ransom, son.

WATSON. What?

MERRICK. Don't get excited. No one's going to mark your
bills.

(**WATSON** *blushes.*)

WATSON. Oh. Yeah, no. Of course.

(**WATSON** *crosses awkwardly to his bag, chucks the
diagnostic tool into it and snaps it shut. Turns back to*
MERRICK.)

So it's gonna be um, eighty-five for the network
problem, and twenty-eight for parts and travel, it's all
broken down on the invoice over here.

MERRICK. Great.

WATSON. So, um. See you tomorrow.

ELIZA. *(from off)* Mr. Holmes!

(At the sound of **ELIZA** *'s voice,)*

*(***WATSON*** becomes* **WATSON.** *)*

*(***MERRICK*** 's office becomes the sitting room of 221B Baker Street, London, 1891.)*

(A desk, three chairs, a small drinks credenza, a cold hearth. Between the three chairs, a low table laid with a light British breakfast and morning papers.)

*(***WATSON*** is on his feet facing the door when* **ELIZA** *sweeps in, in damp, disheveled Victorian traveling clothes.)*

WATSON. Madam.

ELIZA. Mr. Sherlock Holmes, how glad I am to find you in. I am Mrs. Eliza Merrick.

*(***ELIZA*** crosses to* **WATSON** *and shakes his hand firmly.)*

WATSON. It is a pleasure to meet you, Mrs. Merrick, but I'm afraid I am not Mr. Sherlock Holmes.

ELIZA. But this is 221B? The landlady said I should find him here.

WATSON. This is 221B, but Mr. Holmes left our rooms before dawn this morning on the scent of a case, disguised as a hunchbacked Oriental opium fiend. He was quite transfigured, and if our Mrs. Hudson did see him go, doubtless she did not recognize her illustrious tenant. Perhaps I may be of some assistance?

ELIZA. No, I must see Mr. Sherlock Holmes himself.

I require his advice on a matter of some urgency.

WATSON. And you have come a long way.

ELIZA. I have.

(Having gotten one right, **WATSON** *assesses* **ELIZA,** *looking for more clues.)*

WATSON. *(with borrowed panache)* Were he here, I'm sure Mr. Holmes would note that you have traveled this morning from Cornwall – or Brighton perhaps, somewhere southerly – that you have been happily married for many years, and that you are an avid horsewoman – that you visited your stables even this morning, if I am not very much mistaken.

ELIZA. You are mistaken on every count.

WATSON. Ah. Dear me.

ELIZA. I have traveled this morning from Derbyshire, in the north country. I am married, but for somewhat less than a year.

WATSON. *(ever hopeful)* And the stables…?

ELIZA. I have never in my life mounted a horse; I have a dread of them. Do I look somehow, equestrian to you?

WATSON. *(mortified)* No no, it was merely the pattern of mud smears on the hem of your coat that I –

(ELIZA looks down with horror at her traveling clothes.)

ELIZA. *(overlapping; appalled)* Mud smears?

WATSON. Never mind, never mind, I do apologize if I in any way offended in my clumsy guesswork, Mrs. Merrick.

ELIZA. Not at all.

WATSON. I am a student of my friend Mr. Holmes's methods, but I have not a fraction of his native ability, I'm afraid. He may return at any moment, however, and you are welcome to wait. I am enjoying a bit of toast with my tea, if I may offer you –

ELIZA. Thank you, I have neither the patience to sit nor the appetite to eat. I will return at a more propitious time.

WATSON. Very well.

ELIZA. Good day.

WATSON. Good day, Mrs. Merrick.

(ELIZA crosses to exit, but just as she reaches the door she swoons –)

Mrs. Merrick! You are ill!

(– and **WATSON** *rushes to* **ELIZA***, catches her before she falls, and guides her back to a chair.)*

ELIZA. *(woozy)* I am well, no please, I am perfectly well –

WATSON. On the contrary, Mrs. Merrick, you are overcome. I must insist that you stop here and rest until you recover.

ELIZA. Thank you, Mr. –

WATSON. Dr. Watson.

ELIZA. Doctor? You are a physician?

WATSON. Indeed, Mrs. Merrick, and it is my professional opinion that your nerves have sustained a severe shock. Your pulse is visible in your throat; you are pallid where you should be livid and livid where you should be pale. No – lie back, do not exert yourself. I will prepare you a fortifying infusion.

*(***WATSON*** busies himself with the tea.)*

ELIZA. Thank you, Dr. Watson, you are most kind. I do not know what came over me just now; it is quite unlike me to swoon in public. But I am grateful to you for your kindness, and you may prove useful to me after all.

*(***ELIZA*** extends a gloved hand and plucks the fingertips one by one to loosen it before stripping it off her arm with a flourish.)*

In your clinical experience, have you ever come across marks such as these?

*(***WATSON*** crosses to her chair, sets the cup of tea down on the table in front of* ***ELIZA****, and takes her bare hand in his. He examines it diagnostically.)*

WATSON. Extraordinary.

ELIZA. Strange, are they not?

WATSON. May I, I apologize, but may I examine them more closely?

ELIZA. Please.

WATSON. I do not believe my friend will mind if we borrow his glass.

(**WATSON** *crosses to the desk and retrieves Holmes's totemic magnifying glass.* **ELIZA** *yanks her sleeve up higher and thrusts her arm out at* **WATSON.** **WATSON** *peers through the glass at her flesh.*)

Inflamed but not infected. Penetrating at least to the reticular dermis. They appear to be a series of tiny puncture wounds. How did you come by these marks, Mrs. Merrick?

ELIZA. You see, that is what I do not know. These marks are only the latest in a series of singular incidents that have occurred in my household over the past three months – I simply awoke to find them there two mornings ago. I had slept soundly the night before, perfectly undisturbed, but in the morning I discovered my arms dotted like this, on both the right and the left in the same eerie pattern, look.

(*She yanks the glove from her other hand and offers it up. He examines this hand as avidly as the first.*)

WATSON. Yes, they present identically. Pain?

ELIZA. None.

WATSON. Itching?

ELIZA. Too mild to mention.

WATSON. The slight bulls-eye pinking around the center of each contusion is particularly noteworthy. Have you recently been abroad to Constantinople, Mrs. Merrick, or the Hindu Kush?

ELIZA. I have never been east of Dover, Dr. Watson, let alone the Hindu Kush. Why?

WATSON. There is a certain beetle native to Asia Minor that I have seen leave similar traces on its victims' skin. We battled the scourge daily in the field hospitals of Afghanistan.

ELIZA. Even if it were one of our common British midges, the marks are too regular in their spacing, wouldn't you agree? Quite unlike the vagrant pattern of an insect's bites.

WATSON. Indeed, they have a mechanical quality.

ELIZA. Exactly so, Dr. Watson! I ventured as much when I first showed them to my husband, but he dismissed the observation out of hand, and suggested instead that I must have been careless in my needlepoint. In my *needlepoint*, Dr. Watson, a doubly preposterous idea, first of all because no needleworker has ever stabbed herself at precise intervals up the length of her hand and forearm and then *forgotten* having done so, and second because I abhor the domestic arts and have never taken up an embroidery hoop. I do not even own one. After eleven months of marriage I confess it is rather affronting to me that my husband does not know this.

WATSON. Perhaps he was at a loss to account for your strange symptom, and was casting about for any explanation that might reassure you.

ELIZA. I have no taste for baseless reassurance – another thing a husband ought to know about his wife. Truly, his reaction to the marks was as strange as the marks themselves. He could not have been more sanguine about them, and sanguinity is not one of his principal characteristics. Of the two of us, he is the hysteric – too fond, too bold, too loud in his intercourse with the world.

WATSON. Your husband is a passionate man?

ELIZA. Sir, he is.

*(Bright, quick switch to **MERRICK** wrestling with an outdoor ATM machine: a punctuation mark.)*

MERRICK. *Fuck* you 'do not recognize PIN number,' fuck you *fuck* you, I've had this PIN number my entire life you moronic fucking fucking piece of –

(Laser-sharp switch back to the sitting room, no time has passed.)

ELIZA. Though I married him believing him to be quite the opposite. He is a man of science, a noted industrialist. Perhaps you have heard of him: Mr. Frank Merrick?

WATSON. I do not know the name, but –

ELIZA. Inventor of the Merrick Greaseless Piston?

WATSON. I regret that I am wholly ignorant of all things industrial.

ELIZA. No matter. His piston is a turning point in the history of steam engineering, that is all. He is extremely well known among thermodynamic circles.

WATSON. Doubtless, it is only that I –

ELIZA. *(overlapping; continuous)* When I first met my husband I was dazzled by his intellect and his seeming self-sufficiency. He is a genius of angles and equations, a mechanical visionary. I believed that in marrying him I was pledging my troth to a "thinking thing," in the words of the great Descartes. But no sooner had I moved into his home than I began to realize that my husband's mind was little more than an appendage to his large and untutored heart.

WATSON. Ah.

ELIZA. He spends his days in eddies of rages and lusts. He is consumed with the conviction that others are conspiring against him, particularly his former employers, Ransome and Rapier Machinists of Ipswich, who he believes are somehow stealing his ideas. He has gone so far as to accuse me of acting as accomplice to his figmentary enemies.

WATSON. How appalling.

ELIZA. It would all be so farcical if it were not so deeply devastating. I cannot bear to live with a husband who believes me to be so flagrantly disloyal.

WATSON. Your loyalty seems plain to me, Mrs. Merrick.

ELIZA. The longer I am married to him, the less I feel I know him. His moods cannot be predicted from one moment to the next. And when his dark appetites overtake him, he must have satisfaction, immediately, no matter how I may protest –

(she hears herself, stops herself) I have quite spilled my secrets to you, Dr. Watson. I fear I have been indiscreet.

WATSON. No, no, not at all –

(ELIZA *rises.)*

ELIZA. I must go.

WATSON. Mrs. Merrick, you are not well enough yet to go out into the damp.

ELIZA. On the contrary, I am fully recovered, and I have occupied enough of your valuable time.

WATSON. You need not deny your frailty to me, Mrs. Merrick. We all suffer from moments of insufficiency, in which we must look to others to supplement our strength. That is no weakness, it is the first condition of human life. And it is a privilege for me to witness, and minister to, your humanity.

(ELIZA *takes him in curiously.)*

ELIZA. Thank you, Dr. Watson.

(She sits.)

WATSON. Your wrap?

(He relieves her of it.)

Elevate the legs, please, Mrs. Merrick.

(She does, and reclines slightly. He indicates her cup.)

Your infusion.

(She takes a sip. And another.)

ELIZA. Yes.

WATSON. I have added a tablespoon of brandy, for vigor.

ELIZA. Yes, I feel it suffusing me.

(ELIZA *reclines fully.)*

WATSON. Are you quite comfortable now?

ELIZA. Extremely. *(She reclines a bit more fully.)* Just at this moment, I can scarcely recall the urgency of the concerns that brought me here.

WATSON. A series of singular incidents, you said…

ELIZA. They have seemed singular. And they did seem to be in series. But perhaps they were merely a collection of unrelated trifles. Yes, a number of my gloves and underthings have gone unaccountably missing in the past three months. Yes, my husband has recently begun insisting that I join him in a cordial every evening, though I do not drink. Indeed, it was troubling to discover one recent afternoon, under a drape in my private sitting room, a large, sinister device bristling with steel bars, hinged arms, and wax cylinders. But there must be a simple explanation for these things, mustn't there, Dr. Watson?

WATSON. If I have learned one thing from my adventures with Sherlock Holmes, it is that there is no incident so mysterious that it cannot be revealed to have a simple, rational explanation.

ELIZA. Quite right.

(In the distance, the sonorous chime of a clock.)

*(**ELIZA** sits up.)*

My goodness, is it nine o'clock already?

*(**WATSON** consults his pocketwatch.)*

WATSON. It has just gone nine.

*(**ELIZA** is on her feet, gathering her things. **WATSON** rises when she does.)*

ELIZA. I had only planned to stay a moment, and I have let nearly a quarter of an hour go by. At this very instant my husband will be making his way to the Upperton to give his presentation, and I must take care to catch my return train while he is occupied there. He must not learn that I have been here to consult with you. With Mr. Holmes, I mean.

WATSON. The Upperton – do you mean the Upperton Club for Gentlemen, in Pall Mall?

ELIZA. I do.

WATSON. Why, that is my club!

ELIZA. Indeed? Well, you are shortly to be missing there a lecture-demonstration of a striking new device my husband has been seven years at perfecting. I am praying that he will secure at least one investor among the gentlemen in attendance – anything to assuage his inflamed sense of persecution at the hands of the world. My wrap?

*(**WATSON** hands it to her.)*

WATSON. If you can stay even a few minutes more, Mrs. Merrick, Mr. Holmes may return and offer you the satisfaction of analysis that you have not received from me.

ELIZA. I cannot stay, Dr. Watson. And though it is true that you have not offered me the slightest insight into my case, you have supplied me with something of nearly equal value: comfort, and the pleasure of being heard. You are an uncommonly trustworthy soul, Dr. Watson. Your patients are indeed fortunate to have the benefit of your gentle ministrations.

*(She takes his hand. **WATSON** blushes deeply.)*

WATSON. I am gratified to have been of some small service, Mrs. Merrick.

ELIZA. I hope we may meet again, sir. Good day.

WATSON. Good day. Mrs. Merrick.

(She is gone.)

*(For a moment **WATSON** stands still, hands by his sides. Then he crosses to the desk, collects the magnifying glass and a pair of field glasses, tucks them into his medical bag.)*

(He crosses to the door, and, seeing it hanging there on a peg beside his greatcoat, takes Holmes's deerstalker cap

off the wall and puts it on his head. Swings his coat over his arm. Exits.)

(Lights.)

(Tone.)

(Blaze of light up on **MERRICK**.*)*

MERRICK. *(calm, corporate – an executive to his secretary over an intercom)* Mr. Watson, come here? I want to see you.

*(***WATSON** *becomes* **WATSON**.*)*

(Blackout.)

(Lights up on the coffee shop.)

*(***WATSON** *is tailing* **ELIZA** *extremely clumsily – looking at her through binoculars from behind a potted plant or something.)*

*(***ELIZA** *– good boots, cute jeans, nice sweater – watches* **WATSON** *watch her for a beat, and finally approaches him.)*

(He eighty-sixes the binoculars with zero finesse.)

ELIZA. This might seem crazy, but. You're not from the FBI, are you?

WATSON. Who, me? Me? No.

ELIZA. Okay, good.

WATSON. No way.

ELIZA. I didn't think so.

WATSON. You thought someone was following you from the FBI?

ELIZA. Who said I thought someone was following me?

(He's caught. **ELIZA** *shakes her head.)*

I have to tell you. You're a terrible, terrible spy.

WATSON. I'm not a spy, I'm just. I'm sorry.

ELIZA. I feel like I know practically everything about you and *you've* been following *me*. You're like a parade float, you're so conspicuous. Who put you up to this, Frank?

WATSON. Yes.

ELIZA. You a P.I.?

WATSON. Not, not officially.

ELIZA. *(it strikes her)* You're not working on his *campaign* for him, are you? Don't tell me you're one of his PR interns or something. God he's appalling.

WATSON. *(overlapping)* No, no, I hardly know anything about his campaign, just what he told me at his office last week. I only met him cause I work for the Dweeb Team and we've been helping him out with his IT problems.

ELIZA. *(apologetic)* Oh, you work for the Dweeb Team?

WATSON. Yeah.

ELIZA. *(a cross between amused and dismayed for him)* Do you have to, like, show up in the little car and everything?

WATSON. It's like, yeah, it's proprietary, but it's not so –

ELIZA. *(overlapping)* And the giant foam pocket protector? And the novelty glasses?

WATSON. At least as far as the door. But we're allowed to de-gear as soon as we're inside the client's home or workplace. And on follow-up calls we get to skip it. It's not that bad.

ELIZA. I can't believe I actually thought you were FBI. And all the time you were Dweeb Team. I mean, of course, I flatter myself. No one cares about me.

WATSON. *(kindly)* I'm sure that's not true.

ELIZA. No I mean – I don't mean no one *cares* for me, I mean no one cares what I'm up to. I'm not a person of interest.

WATSON. You are to Frank.

ELIZA. I'm not a valuable target for the United States government.

WATSON. *(sleuthing – he ends the line with punch and flair)* But you thought you might be. You had reason to believe you might be, why?

*(**ELIZA** gives him a look.)*

ELIZA. I recently left a sort of high-security job under, ah, less than completely cordial circumstances, and I may have violated my confidentiality agreement by taking a few –. *(pause)* Why am I telling you this?

(She is genuinely mystified.)

WATSON. I asked.

ELIZA. No. *(puzzling it out)* There's something about you.

WATSON. I'm interested.

ELIZA. I don't know what it is. You inspire trust somehow. You're trustworthy.

WATSON. *(pleased)* Really?

*(**ELIZA** considers him.)*

ELIZA. There was this moment last Thursday when I was picking up a new dish drainer at Target, as you know, and I was on my way back to my car and I saw you, like, try to duck out of sight behind a Mini Cooper – behind a *Mini Cooper*, not exactly brilliant cover – and I thought to myself, Oh, there he is again. *(sweetly)* Just – Oh, there's my guy. The one who's been following me. I wonder how he's doing over there behind that Mini Cooper. I hope he hasn't been too cold and uncomfortable out here in this parking lot waiting for me to come out.

WATSON. I was, extremely, cold and uncomfortable.

ELIZA. Well if you were cold you should have said something. I would have given you a ride. Back to my place.

(Pause. They feel things.)

(Lights.)

*(Blaze of light up on **MERRICK**.)*

MERRICK. *(firm, sensuous)* Mr. Watson. Come here. I want to see you.

(Lights.)

(The bedroom.)

(ELIZA and WATSON in bed.)

ELIZA. Well this is new. I've never picked up a strange guy at a coffee shop before.

WATSON. Really? Never?

ELIZA. First time. You're lucky.

WATSON. *(a light correction)* I'm trustworthy.

ELIZA. ...Yeah.

WATSON. I'm just quoting you. You said, "You're trustworthy," at the coffee shop.

ELIZA. Yeah, I remember. It's a little bit weird of you to repeat it back to me.

WATSON. Oh, I'm sorry. I was trying to be, like, precise.

ELIZA. Okay.

(ELIZA gets up.)

WATSON. Where you going?

ELIZA. Um, bathroom?

WATSON. Oh. Okay.

(ELIZA goes off.)

(WATSON gets up. He circulates, looking at things up close that he has only ever looked at from afar until now.)

(calling off) You have a nice place.

ELIZA. *(off)* Thanks.

WATSON. It's hard to believe it used to be a dog food factory.

(Little pause.)

ELIZA. *(off)* Yeah.

(WATSON picks up a framed photograph.)

WATSON. Who's this?

ELIZA. *(off)* Can you, hang on a second? Just – hang on.

(After a moment ELIZA reemerges in yoga pants and a tank top.)

(**WATSON** *lights up.*)

WATSON. *(with the pleasure of recognition)* Oh I *love* those.

(**ELIZA** *looks down, baffled.*)

ELIZA. What.

WATSON. Those pants. You look totally relaxed in that outfit.

(**ELIZA** *nods slowly.*)

ELIZA. Thanks. I guess I...am totally relaxed.

WATSON. *(re: photograph)* Who's this? I could never see – is that you?

(*He shows her the photograph. She takes it into her hands.*)

ELIZA. Yeah, that's me and Mic.

(**WATSON** *takes the picture back, peers at it.*)

WATSON. Where's Mike?

ELIZA. *(points)* There. Oh Mic's not a guy. Mic's a system. M-I-C Mic. He's a natural-language-processing pain management system, for hospitals. He's my doctorate.

WATSON. Oh.

ELIZA. This is him before he got his avatar. He doesn't look like much here. There are versions of him running in six critical care units around Cambridge right now. On site he looks kind of like a pink glowing orb.

WATSON. Oh.

ELIZA. He pulses a little when he's listening.

(*She demonstrates with her hands.* **WATSON** *nods.*)

WATSON. Cool.

ELIZA. I designed him and built him from scratch myself. He was kind of an important milestone in my career. That's why the picture, it's a.

(**WATSON** *nods.*)

WATSON. I get it. He was your first.

ELIZA. Yeah.

(**WATSON** *puts down the photograph.*)

WATSON. You really like your work.

ELIZA. *(no hesitation)* I *love* my work. *(amused)* Is it so obvious?

WATSON. Yeah. And it has something to do with hands?

ELIZA. *(puzzled)* No…artificial intelligence.

WATSON. Oh.

ELIZA. Emotionally intelligent robotics and AI.

WATSON. Oh.

(beat) But so why are you called Digital Fist?

ELIZA. Oh it's a symbol, like a fist, like raised fist? Revolution?

(She demonstrates a revolutionary salute.)

WATSON. So like, robots to overthrow the government?

(**ELIZA** *smiles.*)

ELIZA. No, um… I'm actually just starting out on my own right now, so this is all still in the dream phase for the most part, but I'm developing a device that will support deep Q&A and also be highly sociable, so like, it'll answer any questions you have but it'll also ask you questions of its own, you know, in response to your emotional cues. The core of the technology is based on IBM's Watson, I don't know if you heard about the supercomputer that beat the humans on Jeopardy a few weeks ago?

WATSON. Heard about it.

ELIZA. Yeah so, I was with Watson in the beginning.

WATSON. Cool.

ELIZA. But then I left. And my system is going to be really different – it won't just be a super-enhanced trivia machine.

WATSON. Yeah?

ELIZA. *(moving into her pitch)* Yeah. I'm working on a prototype for a low-cost, high-performance companion unit that will act as a personal advocate for people at the fringes of society. Like low-income people, nursing home patients, disabled vets. These people have been betrayed and abandoned over and over again by the very public institutions that are supposed to serve them. They need reliable, highly skilled, personalized support, a device that can get to know them better and better as it helps them navigate the social services system.

WATSON. Wow.

ELIZA. *(her enthusiasm cresting)* Right? So like, you're poor, you need to go on public assistance. Instead of dragging yourself down to HRA and standing in a dehumanizing line for five hours and getting turned down anyway because you didn't fill out the stupid form right, you activate your companion device before you even leave the house. He retrieves all your documents, analyzes and leverages complex background information for you, and then, because he's fully socially enabled, entertains you if you *do* have to stand in line, and reassures you when he senses that you're distressed. The potential applications are – I mean, unfortunately – endless. People are just plummeting through the holes in the safety net, you know, all over the country, they're literally *dying* for care, and there just isn't the manpower to meet their needs. But with my device, that can all change.

WATSON. *(half to himself)* Amazing. I knew you were –. Amazing.

ELIZA. And of course, social justice is not exactly sexy to multinational corporations. That's why I had to strike out on my own. I want *actual* better living through technology, you know?

WATSON. Oh I get it. I totally get it. This is exactly why I wanted to join the Dweeb Team.

ELIZA. You *wanted* to join the Dweeb Team?

WATSON. Sure, I always wanted to help people, ever since I was little.

ELIZA. But so like, why not be a doctor, or an EMT or something?

WATSON. Um, a lot of the calls I get sent out on are actually just as intense as anything an EMT deals with. You're in people's homes, their system's down, shit gets hairy. There's no telling what can happen on a call.

ELIZA. Wow. I shouldn't harsh on Dweeb Team, I guess.

WATSON. No you shouldn't. We're out there making a difference in people's lives, every day. It's an incredible feeling. Well *you* know what it's like.

(Curious smiles back and forth.)

ELIZA. Hey how did you know I'm called Digital Fist? I don't even have the name on the buzzer yet.

WATSON. *(light)* Building records.

ELIZA. Oh.

WATSON. Do you mind if I ask you kind of a weird question?

ELIZA. Sure.

*(**WATSON** searches for the right words.)*

WATSON. Your ex-husband's so, you know, broken-hearted.

ELIZA. *(dubious)* Yeah?

WATSON. He pretends he's angry at you, but really it's so obvious he just misses you and wishes he could have you back.

ELIZA. *(dark)* So your question?

WATSON. Well…is he right? Are you planning some big move against him?

ELIZA. First of all, it's the height of narcissism for Frank to assume that my plans include him in any –. And you know, I don't really feel like getting into the details of my previous –. And it's sort of weird that you're asking me about –.

*(It sinks in, suddenly, how she met this guy. She makes a little distance between them. **WATSON** objects strenuously under*

the following) You're not reporting back to him about this, are you? *(she gestures – their tryst)* This? Has this all been, like, part of his diabolical plan? Did he send you in here to try to get me to reveal my secrets to you or something?

WATSON. *(overlapping under her previous line)* No, no, no, no, no, absolutely not, no way! No *way!* And Frank didn't send me in here, you *brought* me here!

ELIZA. *(half to herself)* I did. What was I thinking. There was something about you.

*(**ELIZA** begins gathering and handing **WATSON** his clothes, hustling him towards the door.)*

I'm sorry, this has clearly been a huge error in judgment. We should not have done this. You should go.

WATSON. No, please, I shouldn't have brought up your ex-husband, obviously that was a total bonehead move on a first date, of course you're sensitive about him, I should have known that, I *did* know, it was a fuck-up. But don't kick me out, please, not yet.

ELIZA. You have to go, sorry. You have to go right now.

(She all but shoves him out.)

WATSON. Please, more than anything, I just want to give you what you need!

*(**ELIZA** freezes.)*

ELIZA. What?

WATSON. If I'm getting it wrong, just like, nudge me in the right direction!

*(**ELIZA** peers at him.)*

ELIZA. Why are you saying that?

WATSON. Because, because –

ELIZA. Who *are* you?

(A beat.)

WATSON. I'm Josh. Josh Watson.

ELIZA. *(low)* Oh my God.

WATSON. *(stumbling through bashfulness)* I know you think I have some ulterior motive and I can see why you would think that but I just *like* you, I like you. You're very beautiful to me, okay, I think you're a totally amazing person. And this was really good, don't you think? I think we could be really good together. And I know this is probably like, number two on the list of things a person should absolutely never say the first time they get with a girl, but, I feel like I *know* you. I know what you need. I know I can give you what you need.

(He's looking at her very deeply. She can't break his gaze.)

ELIZA. Impossible.

(ELIZA crosses to WATSON. Kisses him.)

(She throws her arms around his neck.)

(They kiss.)

(Lights.)

(Blaze of light up on MERRICK.)

MERRICK. *(a threat)* Mr. Watson, come here. I want to see you.

(Lights.)

(Lights up on MERRICK's office.)

(WATSON stands in front of MERRICK, hands in his pockets.)

MERRICK. You're not wearing your little outfit.

WATSON. I'm not here in my capacity as a Dweeb.

MERRICK. I'm just glad you're here at all. You've been a hard man to reach the past couple days.

WATSON. Yeah, I got a little, caught up in something, so.

MERRICK. It's fine, you're here, and I assume you come bearing evidence?

WATSON. Well –

MERRICK. Go ahead and sum it up for me, the various forms and shapes of the ill my wife wishes to do me.

WATSON. Oh... I don't think she wishes to do you any ill?

MERRICK. Oh yes she does. That's the given. That wasn't the problem I wanted you to solve, that was the given. When she wouldn't take my money, when she wouldn't take any alimony from me at the mediation – of course we had to have *mediation*, we couldn't have a nice erotic cage match in divorce court like normal people – but when she sat there across from me at that table with the fucking mediator and said, "I don't need anything from him. I'll go out with what I brought in," I thought, Oh, I see how's it's going to go. This woman is going to *destroy* me. Not now, maybe, not even in the foreseeable future, necessarily, but she's coming for me. She knows my weaknesses and she has my number and one of these days when I'm not looking in the right direction, boom, she's going to detonate her contempt for me and body parts are going to fly. It's going to be carnage.

WATSON. She seems like sort of a calm person.

MERRICK. *(explosive)* What do you know about her? What do you know?

WATSON. *(backing off strenuously)* Nothing, nothing, just what I've observed for the past few –

MERRICK. *(continuous)* Nothing, that's what you – you can't see it on the *outside*, of course you can't tell what she's made of on the *outside*, but trust me, inside she's nothing but springs and coils of *rage* and *deception* and *scheming* and *hate*. She would do anything in her power to take me down. Anything humanly possible. Who's she sleeping with?

WATSON. *(startled)* No one! No one! No one at all.

MERRICK. *(blazingly confident)* Impossible, of *course* she is.

WATSON. Not, no, not so far as I could tell, no.

MERRICK. Have you *seen* her? She's sleeping with someone, it's just a question of who. That guy from IBM? The co-op guy? One of those fucking fuckers. She made me have that co-op guy over to my house for dinner. I gave that guy food and drink, I made space for him at my table. He claimed to be a black belt in the "peaceful martial art of Ki-Aikido." I said will someone please explain to me what a "peaceful martial art" is? Is that like nonviolent martial law? Guy had no answer for me.

(**MERRICK** *sticks his palm out flat.*)

WATSON. I don't –

MERRICK. *(continuous)* Lemme look at your notes. You took notes, right?

(**WATSON** *adjusts his posture. Takes a deep breath.*)

WATSON. Okay, so, this is the thing. Here's the thing.

MERRICK. *(dubious)* What is the thing.

WATSON. The thing is, I really thought about it a lot, and, you know, from what I could observe this week, she really seems to have moved on. Your ex-wife.

MERRICK. *(highly dubious)* Yeah?

WATSON. She's pretty much doing her own thing now. And I thought, if *I* were still, ah, not totally over someone, and I kept calling them and calling them and they were totally ignoring me and not even listening to my messages anymore, really the last thing I would want would be more excruciating details about what they were up to. I might *think* that was what I wanted, but really it would only be, you know, making things worse.

MERRICK. Look, I didn't hire you to give me your two-bit opinion on my mental state, I hired you to follow my wife!

WATSON. I know, which is why I'm returning your money.

(*From his pocket* **WATSON** *produces a mealy envelope, worn at the corners and fat with cash, that he has clearly been carrying around on his person all week.*)

MERRICK. Jesus – *what?*

WATSON. Well obviously I can't take this. I mean, I didn't do it for the money anyway, I did it because you seemed like you needed a hand, and to be honest I needed a break from my high-pressure job, and even though I'm guessing you're pretty pissed right now, in the end I think you'll see this was the most helpful thing I could do. Because – *(deep earnest)* moving on is so hard sometimes – I mean, I get it, I've been there. It's such a – *(He gestures: fist to his heart.)* you know? And in those moments, when you're in the middle of doing something really crazy and humiliating, what you need more than anything else is a reality check, someone who can reflect you back to yourself, so you can be like, hey, is this really what I want to be doing? Is this really the guy I want to be?

(beat) So that's what I decided to do for you, in the end. I don't think this is the guy you want to be.

(Pause.)

MERRICK. Well fuck you, Deepak Chopra.

WATSON. No, but I –

MERRICK. You're pretty fucking condescending for a Dweeb.

WATSON. No, you're totally misunderstanding me, I'm not saying –

MERRICK. *(overlapping)* We're done here. Gimme that. And get out of my office.

*(**MERRICK** swipes the envelope of money out of **WATSON** 's hand, prepares to usher **WATSON** out.)*

WATSON. But just – think about your campaign, okay? If nothing else? You want to be elected to public office, you can't let people think you're so hung up on your ex-wife that you hired a random dude to follow her to Target! There's no way people are going to vote for a stalker for city auditor!

MERRICK. What – are you trying to blackmail me?

WATSON. What? No! With what? No!

MERRICK. *(overlapping)* I don't know, I don't know what you're *saying* to me!

WATSON. I'm just *saying*, and I'm leaving, okay? But I'm just saying, all that stuff you were talking about, about the government and how we're dependent on it and how it enslaves us and humiliates us, that's good stuff, that really resonated with me! So like, be the change you want to see, right? Your marriage is done, dismantle it. Stop thinking you can rely on her to give you what you need. That's my advice to you and I'm giving it to you for free and I hope that one day you appreciate it. *(beat)* And not that you care anymore, but you have my vote.

(**WATSON** *goes to leave.* **MERRICK** *stands, half-stunned, at his desk.*)

(*Just as* **WATSON** *reaches the door,* **MERRICK** *calls out.*)

MERRICK. Hey, Columbo. How would you know that I've been calling my wife? What did you, spot the caller ID through your night-vision goggles or something?

(*Micropause.* **WATSON** *searches for an answer.*)

WATSON. Phone records.

MERRICK. *(extremely suspicious) You* have access to a private citizen's cell phone records? *Computer guy?*

WATSON. I'm more connected than I look.

(**WATSON** *goes.*)

(*Lights.*)

(*Backstage at the Bell Labs Recording Studio, 1931.* **ELIZA** *briskly preparing* **WATSON** *to go on the air.*)

ELIZA. *(shades of Norma Shearer)* And then the red sign will go on, *(pointing to get his attention)* right up there, and that'll be how you know we're on the air. You've used a microphone before, haven't you, Mr. Watson?

WATSON. *(precise diction, round tones, traces of 19ᵗʰ-Century New England in his voice)* Miss Merrick, I have made a second career of public speaking, on topics as diverse as geology, spiritualism, and the power of the community theater.

ELIZA. Isn't that lovely? Well then, it'll be a simple matter for you to –

WATSON. *(overlapping)* Although no one has ever, until tonight, afforded me the opportunity to share with a broadcast audience the whole story of the birth of the telephone.

ELIZA. Well *whole* story, I don't know about the *whole* story, Mr. Watson, I'm not sure how much our producers told you when they booked you – I just came on here at the Engines of Our Ingenuity program, you see – but I've got eight minutes exactly to give you for the 'phone featurette, because after you we have a radio play coming in about Marconi and his wireless telegraph, so –

WATSON. *(overlapping)* Ah, Marconi. A towering figure in the history of telegraphy.

ELIZA. *(continuous)* – yes indeed, so we'll do our best to get to as much of the story as we can inside the eight minutes. I'll begin by introducing you, then give a bit of background, Bell's biography, your small but crucial role in the process, and then right to the birth of the machine itself, that fateful evening of March 10, 1876 –

WATSON. Yes, they always want to hear about the fateful evening of March 10, 1876. Rarely do they ask about the two hundred and fourteen failed prototypes I labored over for Mr. Bell before that.

ELIZA. And I *do* wish we could hear about every one of them, Mr. Watson, but as I say we'll be hooked off the air promptly at nine past, so I'm afraid it'll just be background, Bell, fateful night in 1876, and then right to "Mr. Watson, come here, I want to see you."

WATSON. Ah, now. If I may, this is significant. What my friend and mentor called out to me in that famous first sentence ever conveyed by wire was "Mr. Watson, come here, I want you." It is often misquoted.

(ELIZA *consults her dossier.*)

ELIZA. I have it here in the notes as "Mr. Watson, come here, I want to see you."

WATSON. Misquoted.

ELIZA. These notes are from the Company.

WATSON. I was the only one there.

ELIZA. Well, after all, it is a minor difference –

WATSON. Yet to me, a crucial one.

ELIZA. (*verging on desperate*) I don't know quite what to tell you, Mr. Watson, I'm merely your interviewer for the evening, and this is only my third day on the job, I'm hardly in a position to –

WATSON. (*overlapping*) The two words that seem to you a minor difference, to me spell the difference between a man calling out to an acquaintance for generalized assistance, and a man calling out to his intimate friend for a service only he can render. I have never misquoted the event, but it was misremembered shortly after it occurred, and it has been resounding through history ever since, accumulating inaccurate implications along the way. I have been striving to set the record straight for years.

ELIZA. Well I'm afraid it's not destined to be corrected tonight. I'm awfully sorry, Mr. Watson, but you do see that our time is short? So I'll say the famous sentence, as written in the notes, then you'll tell the story of the fateful night, in a nutshell, and then describe the prototype for our listeners and demonstrate it live on the air.

(ELIZA *produces a model of the first telephone.* WATSON *regards it with awe.*)

WATSON. Is this – is this the instrument itself?

ELIZA. This is a duplicate, Mr. Watson, but I hope a faithful copy.

WATSON. Extremely faithful. Indistinguishable from the original.

(He picks it up; orates.) Cradling this device once more in my hands, as I cradled it that unseasonably warm night fifty-five years ago in our attic workroom on Beacon Hill, I find myself standing on the threshold of the past, *(he closes his eyes, brings the device to his chest)* hearing my friend's voice call out to me once more with that most heartfelt expression of need...and I am seized with the ancient urge to cry out to him in reply: Yes, Mr. Bell, I hear you, yes!

ELIZA. How wonderful that you recall it all so keenly, Mr. Watson, and we're at time now, so if you could direct that lovely energy right into the *microphone*, please? *(She relieves him of the prototype, points him towards the microphone.)* Marvelous, we're on, then, in 5, 4, 3, 2 –

(A swell of optimistic 1930s radio music.)

*(*WATSON *and* ELIZA *become* ELIZA *and* WATSON.*)*

(Lights up on ELIZA*'s office, evening.* WATSON*, button-down shirt open at the neck, khakis, bare feet, looks slightly down and away from* ELIZA *when he speaks.)*

WATSON. I don't think I understand what you mean, but I'd like to. Can you give me a nudge in the right direction?

ELIZA. *(overlapping)* No I can't, I can't explain it any more clearly than I already have, I'm telling you the guy I'm sleeping with is the living embodiment of –.

(She freezes, overcome with the craziness of it.)

*(*WATSON *waits for a polite beat before prompting her.)*

WATSON. *(warm)* I'd like to hear more about the living embodiment.

ELIZA. Right, no, listen to me, I can't even utter a complete sentence about this. I have these moments where I feel like I see it all so clearly and then a second later I'll be like: what is *wrong* with me? But I just –. I can't explain what it *is* exactly that's so bizarrely compelling about him. I mean on paper, the facts of the case are grim. To begin with, he only owns one pair of pants. One. He goes to the laundromat in his boxer shorts.

WATSON. That sounds funny.

ELIZA. Yeah? That's funny to you? A grown man folding towels in public in his underpants? I would describe that as deeply embarrassing.

WATSON. I'll be sure to keep that in mind.

ELIZA. And that's just the tip of the iceberg. His favorite restaurant is Applebee's. He's a huge, *huge* Billy Joel fan. He went to Medieval Times for his birthday and described it without irony as one of the greatest nights of his life, and yet I can't get *enough* of him, I can't get *enough* of him.

WATSON. That sounds great.

ELIZA. And it's not just the physical attraction. I mean it *is* the physical attraction, the sex with this guy is…

(*She freezes, overcome with memories of their last encounter.*)

(**WATSON** *waits a polite beat before prompting her.*)

WATSON. (*warm*) I'd like to hear more about the sex with this guy.

ELIZA. (*high-pitched, scolding*) Oh I'm sure you would, you perv! Jesus Christ!

WATSON. (*affable*) Sorry. Seems like I goofed with that one. Why don't I take another shot?

ELIZA. (*continuous, cutting him off*) No, first of all, this topic is way, way outside the scope of your comprehension, and second of all it's frankly none of your business. Just drop it.

WATSON. (*amiable*) Sure: Dropping it.

ELIZA. Anyway it's *not* just the sex. It's that…this guy *knows* me. And his learning curve is insane, I mean, I've only been with him a few times and he already knows things about me I didn't even know about myself. Like, the third time he came over he brought me an LED color changing showerhead, I don't know if you're familiar with the technology? You screw it in and it turns your shower into a wet and wild disco, or that's how he described it when he was standing there in my bathtub installing it without even asking my permission. It's actually a pretty ingenious little piece of engineering, and it turns out you can have a pretty great time in there if you turn off the lights and – anyway the *point* is, this is not an item I would ever, ever have brought into my home, and how did he *know*? That I would actually *love* a wet and wild disco shower? It's some kind of crazy predictive algorithm he's running – not just mirroring, it's enhanced, somehow. It's way more sophisticated than anything you can do, buddy, no offense.

WATSON. None taken.

ELIZA. He always knows what I want. Half the time he gives it to me before I even ask. And he genuinely doesn't seem to want anything in return. With Frank, everything he ever did for me was just the opening move of some calculating transaction. This guy is… I would have to describe him as *preternaturally* chill. Purely, perfectly self-contained.

WATSON. That sounds great.

ELIZA. It is. I mean, I don't understand the mechanism. I can't begin to guess how he actually came about. And I know it sounds too I-Robot-y to be real, but I honestly can't think of any other rational explanation for what's going on. There's no way I could feel this way about a normal human guy. And you know what they say: when you have eliminated the impossible, whatever remains, however improbable, must be the truth.

*(**ELIZA** gets a text.)*

(slightly breathless) That's him.

(ELIZA reads the text, shows it to **WATSON.***)*

See? "Meet me @ Applebee's parking lot in 15." And despite everything that has come before this moment in my life, here I go.

(She makes to leave.)

WATSON. Need help finding Applebee's? The nearest Applebee's is on Route 16, in the Susan B. Anthony Shopping Plaza.

ELIZA. *(overlapping, chiming in)...* Susan B. Anthony Shopping Plaza, oh believe me, I know. I've been there twice in the past five days. And I'm not gonna lie: I'm really fucking excited to go back.

(ELIZA gathers her stuff.)

WATSON. You've made thirteen previous requests for me to strike "fucking" from my vocabulary. Strike "fucking" now?

ELIZA. *(grinning)* I have to say, dude, at this moment? I don't fucking care what you do.

(ELIZA exits.)

(Lights.)

(Lights warm on **MERRICK,** *facing out, in his office, after hours.)*

(He grooms himself in an unseen mirror, preparing to speak at a campaign event. Over the following, he combs his hair, adjusts his shirt, puts on and ties his red politician's necktie.)

MERRICK. What I'm feeling right now is a tremendous –. What Americans feel right now is a tremendous sense that their freedoms have been curtailed. Better word. Amputated. Better. Macheted. Macheted through the *neck.* Americans feel that our freedoms have been macheted through the *neck* by a government bent on taxing us to the hilt for what, for what?

To support a zombie army of "public servants" living at our expense, siphoning off the the the *life* juice that folks like you and I produce with our own hands. We're out there working, building things, making things happen, while they sit around with their feet up on desks that *we* paid for, barely putting in eight-hour days, just watching their pensions get fatter and fatter. As long as we keep ourselves plugged into this system, we the taxpayers will get weaker and weaker, while the so-called "servants" grow stronger and stronger. As Ayn Rand says, "The man who speaks to you of sacrifice is speaking of slaves and masters, and intends to be the master." One of my all-time favorite quotes.

(Continuously, as he speaks, **MERRICK** *begins undoing his necktie, unbuttoning his shirt, disorganizing his hair. He begins to groom himself to present at the Upperton Club in Pall Mall: re-combs his hair in the Victorian style, re-buttons his collar, puts on and ties an ascot-style necktie.)*

And that's why I'm running on a platform of total, and complete, individual, liberty. Total and complete independence for every citizen of this once-free nation. Now, I know true independence can feel harsh, especially at first. It can be a real *(he gestures: fist to his heart)*, I get it, I've been there. But it's either tear ourselves free from this system or die mangled in its gears, my fellow Americans! Sometimes the only way to achieve independence is to destroy the thing you're dependent upon.

(MERRICK *is fully Victorianized.)*

(He takes a breath.)

It is a pet theory of mine that you may know a man by the tools he uses, as well as by the tools he does not use. An example: I keep the points on my draftsman's pencils sharp, whittled down as I work until the leads are mere nubs, scarcely long enough to grasp between thumb and forefinger. But the gum erasers on the ends I never touch. Viz, I am precise. I make marks only where I want marks to be, and I do not mark twice.

(From his jacket pocket, **MERRICK** *produces a revolver, gleaming clean. He holds it up for his audience to see.)*

Gentlemen, the tool I present to you today. From a distance it may look familiar, but its interior – you will have a moment to examine it more closely after I conclude – is revolutionary. Like all tools, this one tells a tale about its user. Perfectly shaped to fit a man's hand, it is constructed exactly – and only – to express its master's wishes.

It performs a paradoxical pair of functions: it brings its user and target closer together, allowing a man to pierce the heart of another man from a great distance. And it holds its user and target apart, sparing us the intimacy of carnal combat, the inconvenience of having to come within arm's reach of a foe and club him to death like a savage. Viz, it is a perfect modern instrument.

This particular model, gentlemen, features, in its interior chamber, the miniature greaseless piston I have been seven years at perfecting. This new pistol frees us from the drudgery of powder packing. What's more, it is wedded internally to a calculating machine, a difference engine like Babbage's, but tiny and of my own design, enabling this tool to assess with precision many things we, with our clumsy brains, may only guess at. Targeting. Adjustment. Recoil. Sights. A weapon that knows more, in some ways, than its wielder.

If this instrument intrigues you, gentlemen, let me assure you that it pales in comparison to my even newer device, still too unfinished for public display. The prototype for this very advanced object is currently confined to my private workshop, but the day will soon come when I will reveal it, and usher in a dazzling new era of diminutive mechanization.

I conjure for you a future peopled with miniature machines, in every room of the home, on every street corner and in every shop. Noiseless doors that operate from yards away at the touch of a hydraulic button. Coal-fired hinge-mounted knives that may chop an entire bushel of apples in under an hour. A personal valet made of rivets and plates, whose brass caress, as he fits a man into his jacket, is a thousand times more sure than any boy's could ever be. In an insecure world filled with disloyal people, might we not finally find peace in this Mechanical Garden of Eden, where perfect servants greet us at every turn? What else may be mechanized, sirs, when such devices become commonplace? Where else in the world may we behold this new perfection?

Everywhere around us, gentlemen. Everywhere around us.

(**MERRICK** *slips the revolver smoothly into the inside pocket of his coat. Turns, heads upstage into the dark.*)

(*A train whistle – long, Victorian, shrill.*)

(*In the distance,* **MERRICK** *climbs into a warmly lit train compartment. After a moment,* **WATSON** *enters in his deerstalker cap, climbs into a compartment one window away.*)

(*Blast of steam. The chug of an engine roaring to life.*)

(*Train whistle. Louder, louder –*)

(*–* **MERRICK** *turns back to look at* **WATSON** *–*)

(*Blackout.*)

ACT TWO

(In black.)

(Train whistle – long, Victorian, shrill.)

(– growing closer, closer –)

(– the blast of a steam engine.)

(Night light up on the bedroom, near dark.)

(The rhythmic sound of the steam engine – pistons, clacking cross-ties, rocketing wheels – continues, so loud it vibrates deep in our sternums, as the train rushes North.)

*(In the bedroom, **ELIZA** and **WATSON** have sex.)*

(She is on his lap, their arms are around each other, and they have the strong sensation that they are simultaneously inside each other and fully encompassing one another. From the outside, this looks like virtual stillness, the stunned silence of deep encounter.)

(They hold a slight distance from each other, only so they can witness the incredible thing that is happening to, inside, and between them.)

(It is not a hungry, momentum-driven moment, despite the staccato and roar of the train. It is a timeless moment, in which nothing is happening except a shift in the cosmic order, which from the outside looks a lot like nothing happening.)

*(With both hands, **ELIZA** strokes **WATSON**'s face, his beautiful, transparent face.)*

(She says something to him; he says something to her. We can't hear them over the roar of the engine.)

(They embrace.)

(Darkness.)

(The train subsides into the distance.)

(Quiet.)

(Dark.)

(ELIZA *and* **WATSON** *in bed.)*

(Pause.)

WATSON. … I started out training to be a phlebotomist. But my hand was shaky. In class it's just an orange, nobody gets hurt. But then they placed me in my clinical and I was sticking people and sticking people and they were crying and I was crying… I didn't last a month in the real world. It's too bad, cause I like veins. I like networks and systems. I like to see how things connect, on the inside.

*(***ELIZA** *takes* **WATSON***'s hand.)*

ELIZA. Your hands don't seem shaky to me.

WATSON. Not now. There's nothing in them I could hurt someone with.

*(***ELIZA** *laces her fingers into* **WATSON***'s.)*

ELIZA. I always had a preternaturally steady hand.

WATSON. What does that mean?

ELIZA. "Preternaturally"?

*(***WATSON** *nods.)*

Like…uncanny? Creepy, kind of?

WATSON. Creepy-steady hands.

ELIZA. Like a robot's, yeah. My mom used to have me thread her needles for her when I was like three years old. A thing into another thing – I could always do it.

*(***WATSON** *lifts her hand so it's in front of his mouth.)*

WATSON. Show me.

(ELIZA's eyes widen a fraction. She slips a finger into WATSON*'s mouth. He sucks on it. She closes her eyes. He releases her.)*

(an assessment) Preternatural.

(ELIZA lies with her eyes closed.)

ELIZA. Can I ask you a question?

WATSON. Ask me anything.

(She rolls over and looks at him.)

ELIZA. Are you, are you in love with me?

(WATSON searches his heart.)

WATSON. I think so. Yes.

ELIZA. How do you know?

(WATSON searches his body.)

WATSON. I guess…cause I feel transformed when I'm with you?

ELIZA. Transformed how?

WATSON. I feel…

(WATSON closes his eyes, the better to search his soul.)

I feel open. All the parts of me. My eyes. My whole body. My mind. I weirdly feel like I'm inside you every time I walk past you. Every time we're in eyeshot of each other, even.

ELIZA. Yeah. *(pause)* That's how I feel, too.

WATSON. So we're in love. That's cool.

ELIZA. *(observational)* It is, actually, sort of amazing.

WATSON. Right?

ELIZA. I mean, is it possible that this is it? This is the breakthrough moment, and it's like, for the first time ever in the history of the world this will *work*, it will actually *work*?

WATSON. *(tender)* Why shouldn't it work?

ELIZA. And I will have solved the world's oldest problem, and I will never want for comfort again and you will be my perfect wondrous companion and you will never fail me or leave me alone and I will make a teratrillion dollars off the most profitable invention since the telephone? Can that really be happening?

WATSON. Oh, it's happening. And then we'll take your money and run off somewhere like Tahiti after I finally tell Rick at the Team to kiss my ass and pick up the last of my things from my mom's and you and me can change our names and throw away our phones and spend the rest of our lives lying on a beach sipping alcoholic drinks and having sex under the stars and we can die at the exact same moment in time and be buried side by side in the sand.

(Beat.)

(The facts align.)

ELIZA. Yeah.

(Pause.)

(ELIZA makes some space between them in the bed.)

WATSON. Did I just freak you out or something? I know I can be a little intense sometimes…

ELIZA. *(overlapping)* No. No. I'm cool. I'm fine.

(A beat.)

(WATSON endeavors to close the distance.)

WATSON. Hey. I know you've been through some rough shit. I know better than anyone what you've been through. But I'm different. I totally get that you're your own person. I love that about you. I love you just the way you are.

(ELIZA winces a tiny bit.)

ELIZA. Are you quoting Billy Joel to me right now?

(WATSON grins.)

WATSON. Wow, awesome, I didn't even mean to do that, it just came out that way.

(He nods with wise appreciation.) My man is *relevant.*

ELIZA. Uh-hunh.

WATSON. When you get to know me better you'll see that I'm seriously not about games. What you see is what you get with me, I promise. You can trust me.

ELIZA. *(small)* Thanks.

(Lights.)

(The blasting sigh of a steam engine coming to a halt. Light din of a Victorian country rail station.)

(MERRICK *enters at a brisk stride. A moment later,* **WATSON** *enters.* **MERRICK** *allows him to get three steps into the room, then wheels on him.)*

MERRICK. Indeed, sir? All the way to Derbyshire? All the way to my country station? Fine, then, here we are. Let us have it out, man to man.

WATSON. I, no, I –

MERRICK. *(continuous)* You were shiningly visible in the front row during my speech at the Upperton, then mooning about the corners of the reception hall afterwards like a lovelorn housemaid, then bobbing like a phosphorescent beacon in the night among the crowds on the platform at St. Pancras, then peering preposterously over your Evening Mail from the facing compartment on the four fifteen! You have all the grace and cunning of a typical corporate thug – may I assume you have been sent by my former employers, those rapacious thieves, Ransome and Rapier Machinists of Ipswich?

WATSON. What? No sir, not at all, not at all, I merely –

(MERRICK *begins to tear himself free of his greatcoat.)*

MERRICK. *(continuous)* Very well, sir, I am at your service for a round of fisticuffs, here, now, and the devil take you if I find any patent notes crumpled in your pockets!

(**MERRICK** *comes after* **WATSON. WATSON** *feints and dodges.*)

WATSON. Sir, I do not wish to fight you!

MERRICK. I am not afraid of you, sir! You cut a highly unimpressive figure for a goon!

WATSON. Mr. Merrick, I beg you – I seek no satisfaction through violent means!

MERRICK. Then what sort of satisfaction do you seek, you scoundrel?

WATSON. I merely wish to quench the, the, the *conflagration* of curiosity you kindled in me during your demonstration today! Never in my life have I been so vitally ignited by a man's presentation!

(**MERRICK** *is still dancing at* **WATSON**, *fists up.*)

MERRICK. You are not a patent thief?

WATSON. Sir, I am not!

MERRICK. You are not on retainer with my former employers?

WATSON. Sir, I know nothing about them! I am a complete ignoramus on the subject of mechanics, save what I was able to glean from your speech this afternoon. And of course, what I know about your revolutionary piston.

MERRICK. You know about my piston?

WATSON. Sir, who does not know about the Merrick Greaseless Piston? It is a turning point in the history of steam engineering!

MERRICK. Well, quite right, quite right, though I rarely hear another man say so.

WATSON. I have been appallingly clumsy in my pursuit of you. Truly, I am no gumshoe. But I was tantalized to distraction, sir, by the detail you mentioned in your speech, about an object, stored in your private workshop, so advanced it could not yet be exposed to the public eye. You see, Mr. Merrick, I have recently come into a small inheritance, and I have been looking for an opportunity to invest it in just such a thrilling endeavor as this.

MERRICK. Have you, indeed.

WATSON. I have, sir.

MERRICK. You will forgive me, Mr. –

WATSON. Dr. W – . *(a moment of amateur hesitation)* Dr. Mycroft. Dr. Maurice Mycroft.

MERRICK. You will forgive me, Dr. Mycroft, if I find your explanation somewhat lacking in plausibility. What man tails another man through the streets, lying in wait for the perfect moment to pounce – and offer him pecuniary support?

WATSON. In retrospect I see that I should simply have come up to you at the Club and shaken your hand.

MERRICK. That would have been the traditional method.

WATSON. But I suppose I hoped you would lead me to her.

MERRICK. Who?

WATSON. To it, I mean. To the very advanced object.

MERRICK. Well I have no intention of bringing you to my workshop. No one penetrates the sanctity of my private workshop, not my servants, not even my wife. But it is my habit, when I have been away on an odious journey of self-abasement such as this, to stop at Mrs. Kemp's in the town on my way home. You may join me there for a pint and a pie, if you wish, and I will tell you something about my object. If the description intrigues you, we may begin to discuss an arrangement.

WATSON. I know it will intrigue me deeply, sir. And I would be gratified to break bread with you, having broken your trust so carelessly.

MERRICK. I always need a pint's worth of peace and warmth before I can return to the icy blast of the dinner hour with my wife.

WATSON. Ah. Your wife is a difficult woman?

MERRICK. She is a woman, Dr. Mycroft. Her wiles and wishes are no more a trial to me than Eve's were to

Adam. Though I venture very soon I will be free of her bewitchments.

WATSON. A change is coming to your marriage, Mr. Merrick?

MERRICK. It is, Dr. Mycroft. Imminently, it is.

(Lights.)

(A clock chimes.)

*(**ELIZA** and **WATSON** in her office. **WATSON**, button-down shirt open at the neck, khakis, bare feet.)*

WATSON. You seem anxious.

ELIZA. Anxious? I'm not anxious. I'm a little *distracted*, since he said he would call me to make a plan as soon as he got off work, which should have been thirty-six minutes ago, and I'm unable to go freely about my business until this fucking phone rings.

WATSON. It sounds like that's too fucking bad.

ELIZA. Dude, please, no expletives in your reassurance scripts, okay? That's not soothing. I'm not going to be able to convince the money guys that you're a high-performance companion if you're completely socially tone-deaf.

WATSON. Sorry. Seems like I goofed with that one. Why don't I give it another shot?

ELIZA. *(overlapping)* No no, *I'm* sorry, it's not you, it's me. You're only as good as my input cues, and where have I been to feed them to you?

WATSON. I'm not sure.

ELIZA. Sometimes I think about you here all alone in the dark, with your drives and arousal states stuck in homeostasis, completely at my mercy. Waiting for me to show up and activate you.
(She regards her silent phone. Places it on the mantel, turns her back on it.) I mean it's unconscionable how badly I've neglected you. I don't even know how far along you are now.

WATSON. I'm one hundred percent complete.

ELIZA. Of course you are. Because *you* always do what you say you're going to do.

WATSON. I only want to help in any way that I can.

ELIZA. Can you...help me figure him out?

WATSON. I'd like to try.

(**ELIZA** *shakes her head.*)

ELIZA. He's so intense. He's always looking at me. I can feel him getting closer and closer – it's like he's trying to puzzle me out, trying to solve me like a mystery or something. And I'm defenseless against him. He's irresistibly sexy. And I have no control over anything he sees, thinks, or does. I don't even have control over myself anymore. Sometimes I realize that I've been following him around the apartment, like, trailing after him from room to room all day without meaning to. I think about him all the fucking time. No one has ever gotten this far with me. Ever. And he's just a guy. He's a guy. In a plaid shirt. He's not like you. By definition, he's a threat to the system.

WATSON. Threats to the system should be responded to with deactivation, avoidance routines, or a triggering of the escape response.

ELIZA. Thanks, buddy. That's really good advice.

(**WATSON** *glows a little brighter.*)

WATSON. I'm so glad I could help.

ELIZA. Hey. Why don't you and me do it up old-school tonight. What do we need for a hardcore all-nighter of coding? Break out the old sweats, a little Radiohead, some Smartfood, what else?

WATSON. *(chiming in, eager)* Twizzlers dipped in Jim Beam makes an excellent late-night snack.

ELIZA. Right, buddy. You're the best.

(*On the mantel,* **ELIZA**'s *phone rings: marimba. She freezes.*)

WATSON. *(cheerful)* We're getting a call from 585-637-2219.

ELIZA. Yeah. I hear it. Let it go.

(Lights.)

(Mrs. Kemp's Pie Shop. **MERRICK** *and* **WATSON** *over pints.)*

*(*MERRICK *drinks deeply.* WATSON *sips.)*

MERRICK. A man such as yourself, Doctor, with schooling behind you, a reputable profession – you cannot understand the life of an inventor, teetering on the windswept crag of innovation. I am quite alone, Dr. Mycroft. Forced to cut my own path through the gorse of life. At any moment I may be swept from the height of success into the vale of failure, my bones broken and my fortunes shattered. What's more, I am David to a malignant Goliath, the Messrs. Ransome and Rapier. Years have passed since I threw off the yoke of their corporate enslavement, yet their new mechanisms mirror mine with eerie exactitude. Every hinge, every valve I adjust to my models, they adjust to theirs simultaneously. My mechanical secrets are deeply guarded, Dr. Mycroft, there is no possible way for them to know what I am planning. Yet they *always* know what I am planning.

WATSON. Perhaps – perhaps they came to know the workings of your mind so intimately during your time with them that you exerted a lasting influence on the methods of the entire firm!

MERRICK. Nonsense, Dr. Mycroft, there is a much simpler, more rational explanation. Clearly they have deployed a vast network of spies against me, who dog me at every turn. The mystery is how they manage to slip into my secure workrooms, steal my ideas, and disappear without ever leaving a trace. They are cunning adversaries. But I know they are violating me, daily.

WATSON. How appalling for you, sir.

MERRICK. And worst of all, I am doubted – mistrusted – in my anguish, at the very heart of my domestic life. My wife does not appreciate the seriousness of this crisis. She has begun resorting to sarcasm when I seek her sympathy – recently she suggested with obvious flippancy that I consult *Mr. Sherlock Holmes* to shed light on the situation!

WATSON. But you – . *(He swallows.)* But you do not believe even the great Sherlock Holmes is equal to this case.

(MERRICK considers WATSON with some pity.)

MERRICK. Alas, Dr. Mycroft, you are not one of the credulous millions?

WATSON. I don't understand.

MERRICK. Dr. Mycroft, there is no such person as Sherlock Holmes.

WATSON. Indeed! Is that so?

MERRICK. I have it on good authority that the Holmes the public laps up from those penny-dreadful serials is in fact the artificial creation of his so-called chronicler, Dr. John Watson.

WATSON. Really! Well, really! How remarkable.

MERRICK. It is a rumor, but a substantiated one.

WATSON. But why would he do it? This Watson?

MERRICK. The usual reasons – fame, money, love.

WATSON. Love?

MERRICK. Of course. Ladies love a sleuth. Imagine the passionate letters, the fervent expressions of need and desire, that must flood the postbox of that Watson every day, having dispatched his figmentary detective into the world.

WATSON. Imagine.

MERRICK. Well, and to be fair, it is not only ladies who fall prey to the seductions of "Sherlock Holmes." It is a common enough human wish to yearn for such a figure to be real, a super-endowed mastermind who can answer any question, solve any problem, and ask for nothing in return. His very infallibility is proof that he does not exist. No human being could be as perfectly precise as the Sherlock Holmes we have collectively conjured to life.

WATSON. It is striking to me, Mr. Merrick, that you, a man of science, would question the notion of human precision. Surely the advanced object you are presently to describe to me is itself a quintessence of precise calculation.

MERRICK. By some measures, Dr. Mycroft, yes, but you have hit upon a crucial irony. Facts are critical, but an all-consuming worship of them is, to me, a chilly cult. I never trust a man who trusts only his instruments. What we need from the world should tell us as much about how to design for it as what we are able to calculate about it. Which brings me to my purpose.

WATSON. Ah.

MERRICK. Several months ago I experienced a vision, a momentary blotting out of the mental faculties by passion that resulted, as in a solar eclipse, in a fiery corona of insight. I saw, all at once, that just as machines have brought relief to the coal miner, farmer, and factory worker, they might bring relief to those of us for whom certain psychic exchanges are themselves a kind of labor. There is no end to the work demanded of us in the effort to know another – it is an endless engine chugging away, day and night, in the backmost corner of our minds. And like all inefficient work, it sheds heat in all directions, burning off in wasteful plumes the precious mental energy that those of us who earn our living by our wits require to power our daily activities. My mind is my livelihood, Dr. Mycroft, and I cannot afford to have it ill occupied with the vicissitudes of a baffling but constant interaction.

WATSON. You are referring to –

MERRICK. I am referring, sir, to my wife.

(Bright, quick switch to **ELIZA** *on her phone: a punctuation mark.)*

ELIZA. Hey, sorry I didn't pick up when you called, I was just a little – caught up in something, so. But I was wondering if you could maybe come over later. To talk?

(Laser-sharp switch back to the pie shop, no time has passed.)

MERRICK. It is almost comical to me now, Dr. Mycroft, to think that when I first met the woman who would become Mrs. Merrick, I believed that by marrying her I would relieve my loneliness. I have scarcely felt loneliness so stingingly bitter as the loneliness I have come to know now, within marriage.

WATSON. Mm. Pity.

MERRICK. On this particular day, roughly three months ago, my wife was in an especially recalcitrant mood. I was in the throes of adapting my famous piston to fit the needs of a certain coal mine in Sunderland. The design was eluding me, the deadline was approaching, and my confidence was eroding like sand through a glass. But when I asked my wife if she would sit with me that morning, keep me company in my study so that I should not have to face the fearsome blankness of the drawing board alone, she refused, giving no comprehensible reason, and retired instead to her sitting room to take up her needlepoint, or whatever the devil it is she occupies herself with in there.

WATSON. She does not even – yes, go on.

MERRICK. As I sat at my sketching, tremblingly alone, I began to conceive of a kind of restraint chair I might keep my wife in in the corner of my workshop – exquisitely comfortable, of course, with spaces for books and a table for her to write or work puzzles on, but with clamps here and here for the arms and legs, the better to keep her where I could see her at all times. I abandoned my piston and began to sketch a prototype of this holding mechanism, but as I was inking in the figure to sit in it – I will never forget this moment – I suddenly saw that my wife herself was nothing more than another moving part in my plan. If I might construct a restraining device the rough size and shape of her body to keep her in, very probably against her will, why not do away with the wriggling creature at the center altogether, and construct both wife and chair myself, of a piece. I asked myself: what is it she would be doing in the corner of my room that I would find so soothing? Upon which of her behaviors had I grown so unmanned by dependence? A certain *(he recalls it)* lilt of the voice when she called my name. "Frank, dear." *(he hears it as a song)* "Frank, dear." A Victrola mounted at the head level, furnished with wax cylinders upon which I had etched her voice – captured on a recording device under a drape in her private sitting room – would offer identical satisfaction. Her wifely ministrations would be harder to replicate. She was never the gentlest woman, but there were times when her hand alit on my arm or shoulder as softly as a dove, and the stirring this caused in my heart, Dr. Mycroft, was difficult even to describe, let alone replicate. The hands are truly the most delicate part of the lady, the conduit of all generosity, affection, and care. So the hands. The hands have been my single-minded focus for the past three months, and I have been hard at work on a pair of gorgeous prototypes, a right and a left, that would take your breath away with their sleekness and verisimilitude.

WATSON. I am eager to see them –

MERRICK. Becalm yourself, sir. You will see them when and if we proceed with our arrangement.

WATSON. Of course. *(he thinks a moment)* I suppose, to perfectly replicate your wife's touch, you would need to take an accurate measurement of her hands and forearms.

MERRICK. Indeed.

WATSON. An extremely accurate measurement, with a precision tool of some kind.

MERRICK. Quite right, Dr. Mycroft. An excellent deduction.

WATSON. Perhaps something like…this?

(WATSON goes into his medical bag, which he is never without, and produces a kind of gnarled, forked lancet – a delicate, sinister little metal branch.)

MERRICK. A paralancet! How extraordinary! You have one on your person?

WATSON. I am a medical man, Mr. Merrick. I never travel without my bag.

MERRICK. But a paralancet is a specialist's tool. I ordered my own through an obscure Belgian supply catalog, and I daresay it cost me a pretty penny.

WATSON. *(quiet)* I became quite handy with the instrument in the field hospitals of the Afghan campaign. *(internal)* I should have recognized the marks. They are utterly distinctive.

MERRICK. To map her every tonsure, every one of her ligaments and tendons, I knew I would have to penetrate at least to the reticular dermis –

WATSON. *(overlapping, on "reticular dermis")* Reticular dermis…

MERRICK. *(continuous)* – which might prove quite uncomfortable, even painful, to my wife. So I mixed a sleeping draught into her cordial one night, which served the double function of dropping her soundly into unconsciousness, so I might take my measurements undisturbed, and allowing me to experiment with dosage, for the future.

WATSON. Do you mean –

MERRICK. Well I cannot be sure what I will want to do with her once the prototype is complete and she is fully replaced. It is a bit of a conundrum for me, in fact. I scarcely relish the thought of disposing with

her completely – after all, Dr. Mycroft, I *love* her, and
I have no small affection for her soft, comely body
which is its own delicious torment to me. I did think of
keeping her in a permanently somnolent state, dosing
and re-dosing her in cycles before she could wake, but
that seems needlessly custodial.

WATSON. Perhaps, Mr. Merrick, you could simply let her
go. Free her to find her happiness with someone else.

(**MERRICK** *considers* **WATSON** *with mild suspicion.*)

MERRICK. That option holds no particular interest for me,
Dr. Mycroft.

(**WATSON**'s *hand closes tightly around the paralancet.*)

WATSON. And if she suspects you? And tries to foil you?

MERRICK. She may well suspect me, Dr. Mycroft, she is no
fool, but she –

WATSON. *(cutting him off)* If she takes bold action on her
own behalf, and travels to London unbeknownst to
you, and makes the plight of her blighted marriage
known to someone who feels for her, and is willing to
sacrifice for her, and very possibly has the power to
save her?

(**WATSON** *gets to his feet, clutching the paralancet.*
MERRICK *remains seated.*)

(*Pause.*)

MERRICK. I believe you have been charmed by some
flight of fancy about yourself, Dr. Mycroft. You seem
to be acting a role – the hero of an imaginary gothic
romance you are even now authoring in your mind.
I'm sorry if this offends you, but you are plainly no
hero. We have enjoyed a friendly enough chat, but I
do not believe you have as much to offer me as you
implied.

WATSON. *(hoarse)* Mr. Merrick, I cannot allow you to hurt
her.

(WATSON attempts to menace MERRICK with the paralancet, but the hand in which he holds it trembles violently.)

MERRICK. Dr. Mycroft, your hand is shaking.

(In a swift movement, MERRICK stands and seizes WATSON's hand, steadying both hand and instrument in his powerful grip.)

Release the paralancet, Dr. Mycroft.

WATSON. *(his voice breaking)* Never, sir.

MERRICK. *(easy)* Dr. Mycroft, kindly do not force me to use my relaxed free hand to grasp the powerful weapon of the future you very well know is at the ready in my waistcoat.

(MERRICK pulls the curtain of his coat on the revolver. WATSON witnesses it; WATSON yields.)

I am sorry, because it is expensive, but I must relieve you of this for my own safety.

(MERRICK pockets the paralancet handily.)

Now. You will leave Mrs. Kemp's at once and proceed to the southbound platform of our country station. Your return train will arrive in roughly eight minutes. You will board it, settle comfortably into a compartment, and allow yourself to be conveyed home to London, never to return to Derbyshire again.

WATSON. But, I –

(MERRICK exits.)

But I…

(Lights shift.)

(WATSON turns.)

(WATSON becomes WATSON.)

(The bedroom.)

(ELIZA and WATSON, edge of the bed.)

I don't get it.

ELIZA. I know you don't.

WATSON. Do *you?* Do you get why you're making the stupidest move of your life?

ELIZA. Of course I do.

WATSON. No you don't. You can't. You're the smartest person I know. There's no way this is what you mean to be doing.

ELIZA. It's what I have to do.

WATSON. Why?

> (*nothing from* **ELIZA**)

Look at me.

> (*nothing*)

Look at me.

> (**ELIZA** *turns to look at him.*)

Why?

ELIZA. I can't explain it to you.

WATSON. This is a kind of paradise of awesomeness that we were lucky enough to stumble into by accident, and now you're like, okay, enough, I've had enough of paradise, I can't explain why, you can stay here by yourself if you want to but I'm done, I've had all the paradise I can take.

ELIZA. It doesn't feel like paradise to me.

WATSON. Oh yeah? Which part? The seven-hour sex marathons? The crazy amazing mind-meld where we practically know each other's thoughts before we think them? The perfect sweetness of looking at you and knowing that you see me exactly as I am?

ELIZA. All of it.

WATSON. Okay well so that's love. That's called love.

ELIZA. Maybe.

WATSON. No, *definitively*, those are the definitive qualities of love. You're saying you don't want love?

ELIZA. I don't know.

WATSON. What is wrong with you?

ELIZA. I don't know!

WATSON. Is this, like, some kind of fucked-up low-self-esteem thing left over from junior high?

ELIZA. *(overlapping)* I highly doubt it.

WATSON. *(continuous)* No, no, it can't be that, you have ridiculous amounts of self-esteem, you're the bossiest person I've ever met and not hated. Wait – it's me. You think I'm not good enough for you.

ELIZA. *(overlapping)* No no no, not at all, not at all! You're exquisite, you're a masterpiece, you're the most magnificent creature I've ever laid eyes on.

WATSON. *(overlapping)* I'm a Dweeb and you're a Ph.D., you're still hung up on that meaningless bullshit. I'm too nice. I'm not an asshole like your ex-husband and you only like assholes. You don't like the 'stache. You don't like the 'stache? I'll shave the fucking 'stache!

ELIZA. *(overlapping)* No, no, no.

WATSON. No you know what? I *won't* shave the 'stache, I won't shave it because it's actually an important part of who I am and I am the one who loves you and you're lucky that I do, and that I'm willing to put up with all the painful shenanigans you're putting me through, and I will not deny you the privilege of being loved by me, 'stache and all.

ELIZA. I think you're acting a little irrationally.

WATSON. Oh, *I'm* acting irrationally? *I'm* acting irrationally? You're the one breaking up with me for no comprehensible reason in the middle of the greatest love affair of our lives, and I say to you: No. Fuckin' no. Deal with *that.*

ELIZA. You don't get to say no.

WATSON. I don't "get" to say no? It's a free country, baby, I get to say whatever I want!

ELIZA. *(sharp, rising pitch)* This is it, okay? *This* is it, I can't *do* this!

WATSON. What? What?

ELIZA. I can't figure you out! The longer I know you the less I understand you! I never have a clue what you're going to do next!

WATSON. Oh yes I'm a wild man! I'm liable to do anything! I could leave Route 16 one exit early and drive through a Blimpie's! I could make us rent Maid in Manhattan at Hollywood Video!

ELIZA. No, but I mean –

WATSON. *(continuous)* Don't you *know* me by now? I'm the most predictable dude you will ever meet and you're cutting me loose for being too wild?

ELIZA. Look. I can't make you understand this. I don't know why I'm even trying. It's way, way outside the scope of your comprehension.

WATSON. *(cold)* Why don't you fucking try me.

*(***ELIZA*** breathes.)*

ELIZA. You're too perfect and you're too imperfect. You're the only one I want to be around, and I have a really hard time being with you. When I'm with you I feel like I can't breathe, and when I'm away from you I feel physically sore, here, like someone punched me extremely hard in the chest. I feel destroyed, I feel – dismembered, sort of, or maybe it's the opposite, I feel so incredibly, powerfully coherent that I'm about to implode from the pressure, I don't know, I don't know, what have I let you do?

WATSON. Baby –

ELIZA. *(continuous)* I could feel you working your way inside me. And now you're all the way in, here, right here against my heart, like a little hot stone, and there's nothing I can do about it anymore, but what are you going to do to me now that you're in there? You could do anything. You could poison me. You could tear me open. You could detonate and shatter me into a thousand pieces. You could disappear and leave me empty and alone.

WATSON. Baby, I would never –

ELIZA. *(overlapping; not listening to him)* I can't trust anything anymore, not even my own body. There's no part of me you haven't touched.

(WATSON comes to her.)

WATSON. All I want to do is love you, and give you what you need. How can you think I would do anything, anything to hurt you?

ELIZA. I *know* you're going to hurt me. In fact, you're hurting me right now.

WATSON. Okay, I. I mean, Jesus. Okay.

ELIZA. I'm sorry.

(WATSON stands.)

WATSON. *(quiet now)* I really wish you wouldn't fucking do this. You're going to be so sorry. And I'm not like you, I can't just flip a switch and –. I'm not going to be able to just pick up again where we left off, someday down the road when you finally get your shit together.

ELIZA. I know.

WATSON. This is it. This is your chance. Tell me not to go.

(ELIZA doesn't look at him.)

ELIZA. I can't. I'm sorry. *(pause)* Go.

(Lights.)

(Tone.)

(ELIZA alone.)

Watson.

Watson. I don't –.

Watson I can't –.

Please, Watson.

Watson, come back.

Watson, come back, I want –

Watson, come here, I want to see you.

Watson, come here, I want you.

(A swell of optimistic 1930s newsreel music.)

(A recording studio in Bell Telephone Labs.)

(**WATSON** *and* **ELIZA.**)

(The red ON-AIR light is on.)

WATSON. *(pleasantly surprised)* Well, that's right. Thank you, Miss Merrick, for your accuracy. That famous sentence, as you know, is often misquoted.

ELIZA. *(dazed)* Did I…?

WATSON. *(the round tones of a well-rehearsed story)* So it was that my friend and mentor Alexander Graham Bell, having set up the transmitter in his work room, and having sent me with the receiving instrument several rooms away, nothing linking us but twenty yards of wire, was preparing to make a test of the machine, when all of a sudden, a rapid motion of his arm upset a battery jar of acidulated water onto his clothes, and, urgently needing my assistance, he called out to me: "Mr. Watson, come here, I want you!" And I heard every word through the wire – clear as a bell, as I have often said, humorously.

ELIZA. Can I ask – how did you handle being so dependent on him?

(**WATSON** *is mildly startled.*)

WATSON. I – well, my goodness. I never thought of myself as merely dependent. We were intimately connected. Over time, I had transformed myself into a sensitive instrument, allowing myself to grow into the peaks and valleys of my friend's needs, learning what he preferred and what he disliked, when to come towards him and when to recede. Thus was I able to create the optimal conditions for his world-changing ideas to flourish.

ELIZA. But that must have been so humiliating for you, giving yourself over to him like that.

WATSON. I would not describe it as humiliating, no. The ability to contribute selflessly to an endeavor larger than oneself is, to me, a precious gift. And naturally, I enjoyed the quiet pleasure of knowing that I was indispensible to the process. My Bell, you see, was a visionary, but a clumsy man. He could never have constructed those two hundred and fourteen prototypes without my skilled hands at his disposal.

ELIZA. *(urgent)* But – it must have been so *excruciating* for you to connect with him and then –. I mean now that he's gone, you're *nothing* without him. You'll never be just yourself again, always Watson to his Bell.

*(**WATSON** breathes.)*

WATSON. When one is small, Miss Merrick, when one is coming up, one learns about the extraordinary people, people who have made their mark on history and done something noteworthy for mankind, and naturally one assumes that one will become such a person, since those are the only kinds of people one reads about. One thinks, surely I'll be the next Copernicus, or the next Abraham Lincoln, or the next George Bernard Shaw. It doesn't occur to one to question this. Then as one grows older one comes to see that the interesting people, the ones who have made their mark on history, are in fact surrounded by a halo of shadowy figures, other less extraordinary people whose role it has been to help the extraordinary person make his mark. Assistants, transcriptionists, secretaries. Wives. And though occasionally one of these shadowy figures will find him or herself, long after death, plucked from obscurity and biographized by some eager young scholar with a soft spot for underdogs, by and large their names have all been lost, their stories rusted away in the rain, not having been sheltered by the awning of history like the stories of the extraordinary people. And as one gets older one comes to realize that there are a great many – *great* many – people in the world, far too many for all of them to go down as extraordinary, and anyway one sees that not everyone *is* extraordinary, one comes to understand that one is oneself in fact not all that terribly thrilling or unusual, but that one does have the capacity, the particular set of traits and skills, it would require to help a thrilling person make his mark. And though naturally this realization may engender a certain bitterness, *(swallows)* if one is at all clever or mature one makes the best of this lot. Surely, one accepts if one is at all mature or clever, one is, in fact, lucky.

ELIZA. *Lucky?*

WATSON. Yes. It is always a stroke of luck to connect with another, even briefly. Even if the outcome is difficult.

ELIZA. But I don't –. I don't know if I can *bear* it. It's such a *(she gestures: fist to her heart)*, you know?

*(**WATSON** nods.)*

WATSON. Connection isn't elegant, or precise, or rational. But it's our fate to be bound up with one another, isn't it. We are all born insufficient, and must look to others to supplement our strength. That is no weakness, it is the first condition of human life. *(It strikes him.)* Why, the very success of the telephone is evidence of this need. If we did not rely upon each other so deeply, our nation would not now be strung like a vast, glittering web with eight million miles of connecting wire.

*(**WATSON** gazes out at the web of connection, glittering as far as his eye can see.)*

*(**ELIZA** peers desperately in the same direction, seeing nothing.)*

*(After a moment, **WATSON** moves on.)*

And now I see that our time is up, and we must cede our hour upon the stage to the great Marconi, whose revolutionary device –

ELIZA. But no, please don't go – will you – demonstrate the prototype? For our listeners?

(Gentle shift.)

(WATSON *becomes* **WATSON.** *)*

WATSON. Yeah, no. I guess I can't explain this in a way you can understand. And I really can't do this anymore.

(WATSON *hands the prototype to* **ELIZA.** *)*

You have to figure it out for yourself.

(WATSON *disappears.)*

(ELIZA *watches him go.)*

(Pause.)

(ELIZA *examines the instrument. She struggles to place a call.)*

(First ring: jangly – wall-mounted phone box.)

(Second ring: shrill – midcentury rotary.)

(Third ring: digital – 90s cordless.)

(Lights up on **MERRICK.** *)*

(Fourth ring: the xylophone tone of a smartphone, coming from the phone in **MERRICK** *'s hand. He answers it.)*

MERRICK. Hello.

ELIZA. Hey. It's me. I want to see you.

(Lights.)

(ELIZA *and* **MERRICK** *alone together.)*

(ELIZA *on the couch.* **MERRICK** *sits opposite, in* **WATSON** *'s spot from the first scene of Act I.)*

ELIZA. I was wondering how you were.

MERRICK. I'm fine. I'm pretty good.

(Pause.)

I've been… I built a shed.

ELIZA. Oh yeah?

MERRICK. I put up a – one of those pre-fab, from Lowe's.

ELIZA. Under the oak tree?

MERRICK. No, over where the leaf pile was.

ELIZA. That's nice. That's a nice place for a shed.

MERRICK. For tools.

(*Pause.*)

ELIZA. How did your campaign go?

MERRICK. (*incredulous*) Are you kidding? I won, didn't you see the results? I won.

ELIZA. Congratulations.

MERRICK. We had a great little election night party at Dinino's, I wish you could have been there.

ELIZA. Yeah.

(*After a beat,* **MERRICK**'s *eyes narrow.*)

MERRICK. Did you even vote?

ELIZA. I meant to.

MERRICK. You didn't *vote? You* didn't vote? I can't –. I can't –. If you couldn't bring yourself to vote for me, fine, you could have voted for Capistrano or Sawicki, but you didn't even *participate?*

ELIZA. I would have voted for you. I think.

MERRICK. What, you didn't have time that day? You were booked solid and couldn't squeeze it in? I can't believe you didn't vote!

ELIZA. I had kind of a lost weekend. That lasted a couple of months.

MERRICK. What happened?

ELIZA. How's the job so far? Is it everything you dreamed it would be?

MERRICK. Well it's a colossal clusterfuck, naturally.

(**ELIZA** *smiles.*)

I mean I don't officially take office until the new year, but I can already see it's going to be a colossally titanic clusterfuck. For one thing it's going to be twenty-four-seven the first couple of months and I don't know what that's going to mean for my practice, but I have to keep the practice because do you realize what the salary is attached to this position? Twenty-seven thousand dollars a year. To take total fiscal responsibility for an entire city, twenty-seven thousand dollars a year. They *expect* you to keep your private-sector job, they *need* you to keep it, while you somehow also manage your full-time responsibilities to the city, county and state, otherwise how could you live? It is not possible to live on twenty-seven thousand dollars a year. Not with a mortgage. Not with car payments, not if you want to eat fresh produce and pay a professional to keep the back of your hair from growing over your collar like a goddamn beatnik. So I don't know how it's going to go, practically. But I'm going to roll up my sleeves. I'm not afraid.

ELIZA. I can't believe you'll even touch their twenty-seven thousand. That's taxpayer money, you know.

MERRICK. Look, I'm not a saint.

ELIZA. *(smile)* No kidding?

MERRICK. I'm not going to take a second full-time job rooting out waste and abuse in my city out of the goddamned goodness of my heart, that's not happening, I require at least *symbolic* compensation for what promises to be a Herculean task. I have already – the *morning* after the election, I was still buzzed on Dinino mojitos and I'm already getting emails from your various interest groups, seven, eight in the *morning* the day after the election. Alan Winkleman from St. Jude's Hospital and Mary Anne what's-her-name from the district library system and Jim Threadwell from the law enforcement unions, just "reaching out," just "reaching out to congratulate me" and hoping to set up a meeting – every one of these charming parasites is gonna want a meeting and every one of them is gonna want to shake my hand, and they think if they touch me, if they show up in my office and put their hands on me and look deep into my eyes and tell me a bunch of sob stories about this kid's got cancer and this Somalian refugee needs to learn how to read and this injured cop's got a family to feed, I mean, okay, maybe that one, possibly, but on the other hand they're mostly out there directing traffic, as a law-abiding citizen that is my main interaction with the police force and half the time they can't even be bothered to *direct* the traffic, they're out there in the intersection in their little vest and whatnot but they're not even gesturing, or they're gesturing so vaguely you have to roll down the window for clarification, and what are orange cones *for*, after all? Can we as citizens not understand the meaning of a line of orange cones, do we really need a human being out there pointing like a scarecrow on full municipal salary and benefits? I lost my train of thought.

ELIZA. They think if they come in and shake your hand –

MERRICK. *(overlapping; picking up the thread)* – If they shake my hand and make some kind of human connection with me I'll be like, okay, fine, you can keep your precious pediatric oncology unit, okay, okay, just stop showing me pictures of the sick little kids with all their hair fallen out and their little bruised faces...

ELIZA. They're already showing you pictures of kids with cancer?

MERRICK. That Winkleman is a fucking asshole, the *morning* after the election, the guy is fucking shameless. I had to delete the email from my inbox, it was like a punch in the gut. They're having a Christmas party in the picture. Little bald elves. Whatever. I'll meet with him. See what he has to say for himself.

*(*ELIZA* nods.)*

How's your what, your startup?

ELIZA. Extremely good.

MERRICK. Naturally.

ELIZA. I went into my big venture cap meeting at Pearson Klein with zero expectations, all but hallucinating for reasons I won't go into, wearing the shirt I'd slept in, left my prospectus at the office, didn't even bring the prototype, and they practically went down on me they were so excited about it.

MERRICK. And you let them, of course.

ELIZA. Let them, let them capitalize phase two? So I can outsource some of the tedious coding and make rent without getting a cash advance on my credit card? Yes, I let them.

MERRICK. You must be very proud.

ELIZA. They said they've just been waiting for something like this to walk through the door. This is the world we want to live in, apparently, where every device we touch supports user-directed mirroring interactions. And my work with Watson *(she swallows)* makes me uniquely positioned. They said to backburner the part where it's an instrument of social justice. Let the market drive use and placement, they said. It'll find its niche.

MERRICK. Chomsky must have rolled over in his grave at that one.

(Little pause.)

ELIZA. Yeah. Chomsky's not dead.

MERRICK. *(extravagantly apathetic)* Whatever.

(Pause.)

*(**ELIZA** looks down. **ELIZA** speaks carefully.)*

ELIZA. I've missed you.

*(**MERRICK** raises his eyebrows.)*

MERRICK. You have, huh.

ELIZA. I wanted to say that it was wrong for me to cut you off like that. I didn't know.

MERRICK. What?

(**ELIZA** *searches for the words.*)

ELIZA. How you were feeling.

MERRICK. I don't believe I was shy about expressing myself.

ELIZA. No, but I didn't understand then.

MERRICK. Uh-hunh. So...what?

ELIZA. So I apologize. And I hope you accept my apology.

(**MERRICK** *nods thoughtfully.*)

MERRICK. Well I don't know. I don't know, you kicked me around like a deflated soccer ball for ten months, now you want me to accept your apology?

ELIZA. *(starting to fray around the edges)* I didn't mean to kick you around, honestly, I was trying to do the exact opposite of kicking you around, but you were so difficult about – look I really don't want to get into it all again, I just apologize, can I just apologize to you and have you accept it? Is that so fucking impossible, Frank?

MERRICK. What happened to you? I didn't want to lead with this but you don't look so good, Lize. You look a little flattened.

(**ELIZA** *nods. She endeavors to keep it together.*)

ELIZA. Can I ask you...sort of a weird question?

MERRICK. Shoot.

ELIZA. What did you do? After I left and you were all –. How did you – ? What did you *do*?

MERRICK. Uh well, lemme see. I descended into the first circle of hell and started to make, let's call them uneducated choices about how to behave towards you.

ELIZA. Yeah.

MERRICK. I focused all my energy on destroying you so I could free myself from your relentless heartless indifference. Then, I don't know, that didn't work, and it was taking up a lot of my time and energy, so I descended a little further into hell, and then a little further and a little further then finally all the way down to the bottom of hell, and I kept trying to call you the whole time, I kept calling you and calling you trying to be like, Excuse me, please pick up, I'm calling from hell, can you please take my call because I'm calling from hell? And I couldn't believe you wouldn't answer. But then finally I realized that *no one* can take the calls you place from hell. People can't even hear it ring when you call from down there. Service is blocked or something. So *that* whole idea kind of landed on me like a ton of bricks, and after that I just kind of sat around for a long time down there on the ground, just beholding Satan's red eye and watching the walls bleed and roasting in the hellfire and whatnot, and then eventually I, I don't know.

ELIZA. Yeah.

MERRICK. I was thinking about writing a book about it, actually. After my term is up and I'm not such a visible public figure. Like, a man's guide to getting over his ex-wife. With tips, and it could be shelved in the sports section or something, someplace people wouldn't have to compromise their dignity to go into.

ELIZA. I'd buy it.

(pause)

MERRICK. *(subdued)* So who was it, in the end? The guy from IBM? That co-op guy?

ELIZA. Your guy.

MERRICK. *My* guy? Which one's *my* guy? *(It hits him.)* Wait, the *computer* guy? No way!

*(***ELIZA*** nods.)*

You've gotta be fucking kidding me, *that* guy?

*(***ELIZA*** nods.)*

You're telling me I spent our entire marriage inventing paranoid fantasies about you cheating on me with every guy that walked past us and in the end I *sent* him to you? Right into your arms?

(**ELIZA** *nods.*)

Well fuck me. I guess I was absolutely determined to be right about you.

(**ELIZA** *nods.*)

ELIZA. It's so unbearable. But it's also amazing. I can feel everything, all their hope and despair and need. We're sharing a drink we call loneliness, but it's better than drinking alone. In the words of the great Billy Joel.

MERRICK. ...What?

ELIZA. I just mean, I'm connected to them. Other people. Everywhere around us. Everywhere around us.

(**MERRICK** *and* **ELIZA** *look at each other.*)

(*They look out at everyone else.*)

(*Lights.*)

End of Play